SINGER IN THE NIGHT

PART ONE

Letters to loud lovers

'Here at last is a true lover,' said the Nightingale. *'Night after night have I sung of him, though I knew him not: night after night have I told his story…'*

WELCOMING LETTER

Dear citizens, householders, close friends, fellow townsfolk, mild and attentive civil servants and waiters, courageous and patient nurses, magicians' secretaries, dressers of abundant hair, eternal children in short trousers, seasonal ice-cream sellers, dealers in intoxicating substances, drivers who brake on bends, gondoliers of urban orbits, captains on foreign ships, foreign girls on captains, neighbours – agreeable disco gladiators, neighbouring proto-astronauts and everyone else in Dinko Šimunović Street, not to list you all,

I am writing because before I leave I want to tell all of you that we live in the loveliest street, in a wonderful city, in a country without match or peer!

The sun rises at five, warms us, and sets at eight, sometimes at nine, and at night, without our knowing it, cascades of meteors pour over our heads, while down below, in front of our doorways gleam the little golden stars of apartment bells, caper flowers close their calyxes filled with heady aroma, and the quiet air refreshed by nocturnal moisture is riven only by lovers' cries. Summer in the city is rainy and hot and plants from ground-floor gardens beside the root and trunk of skyscrapers grow as far as the birds, up to the tenth or fourteenth floor. Some may find that monstrous, but it's beautiful. Towards evening, cats awaken, and go scampering along the branches of the climbing plants, they fly over the narrow sky-filled gaps between apartments, with the occasional curse flying after them, which makes the image real and protects us, up to a point, from madness.

It may be like this also in other towns on the meridian and further afield, but do they have such tall and proud men, modest champions with powerful thighs and such well-built women with ponytails and long nails, somewhat impudent, in the way that a thorn on a rose or bramble by the road is impudent, do they have such aromatic pines constantly under their city windows, such melodious voices, such healing sea and such a street, a cheerful torrent, a musical ladder, a flight of steps travelling into future memories, into incorruptible childhood? And are they aware of it?

Because, if you do not know how lucky you are, then you really are out of luck. Enjoy it all, even unthinkingly!

With love from your neighbour,
Nightingale,
35 Dinko Šimunović Street.

Two weeks had passed since that event, and I had set out in search of the man who wrote the letter. After a brief visit to Split, I decided to turn off the motorway onto a side road and to speed off into that steppe-like landscape where even a goat would go hungry, towards his native village.

Even then I was aware that I was finding it increasingly hard to concentrate and that my thoughts were slipping away. I could not recall the meaning of a road sign: a consequence of my state of mind, or perhaps ordinary emotional excitement. (Maybe both). That's why I'm going to record them – those thoughts and letters – so that my notes about everything that was happening or was going to happen in connection with all this would remain preserved for me (primarily for me, yes) and maybe for someone else, my dear.

Mitrovići, Nightingale's village, in the hills where the frontiers of Croatia meet Bosnia and Montenegro, has a small U for the Croatian Ustasha and a sticker of the Hajduk football club logo stuck beside the name of the village, above the name is a stop sign – you have to stop (although there's never anyone there) before continuing on your way.

His mother met me in front of the bell-tower plonked in the middle of the village. The clock on the tower, black hands on stone, was fifteen minutes late and pointed to midday. She was alone, she and several flies, and she had not sat down but, large and round as she was, she was rocking from one foot to the other. She had wrapped a black scarf with bright pink roses on it round her head: her face blossomed into a smile when she caught sight of me. The beginning of September is hot, but not in that lethal

July way. September is summer after ecstasy, lazy, stupefying and discreetly illuminated in the moment before everything that has just ripened begins to rot. Everything has been brought to its height, in tastes and colours, and then subdued into an over-rich tenderness, melancholy.

She said 'Bloody 'ell you looks great, better than on telly!'

She said that and kissed me on both cheeks, then took my arm and led me into the house on the square.

I looked dreadful, after two days' driving with a broken air-conditioner (the fact that the car is a convertible didn't help) and after I'd been peed on by a dog, but I didn't say so, after all that I was glad of that moment, that compliment.

'Nothing from Gale,' I say, taking out his last letter. 'I was given this by the lad who's looking after his flat, living there. (I didn't mention the other letters.)

She took a carob pod out of her apron pocket and chewed it. Then offered me another. 'More scribbling, damn 'is eyes. I can't read it any more. So tell me – no one knows where he is. What do we do now? How're you going to find him? And what if he's not in Bosnia? You'd do better not to look for him.'

She's called Josipa, Nightingale's Mum.

She flapped her hands over her thighs a few times – I shrugged my shoulders. 'Don't worry, my dear,' I say. 'I'll find him. The world is limited, but time is infinite.'

She looked at me quizzically as though I had spoken in Chinese and swatted something with her hand.

'It's a quote from a graffito, my dear. Gale wrote it,' I say. I didn't want her to think I was making fun of her. I felt stupid and in my awkwardness I downed in one gulp the brandy she had poured for me.

She put her hand out towards the letter. 'So, let's have a look!'

She read slowly, her lower lip forming the letters.

'He had put it in all his neighbours' letterboxes before he went away, instead of saying goodbye I suppose.'

'It always surprises me, what he writes. But I can't make anything of this. Is he sick, what do you think?'

I shook my head.

'I'm glad he's okay. Since when does he love Split?'

'Sorry?'

'In the letter he loves Split. He didn't like it much before, he didn't even go out, except at night like a fool.'

She squinted at me and the roses on her head shook.

'He was never completely normal, ever since my late husband gave him the name Nightingale, I would have called him Daniel or Petar. We were old when he came along, maybe that's why he's like he is. It's shameful in the village, me having a child at forty-two and my man a whole sixty years old. Our neighbours were getting grand-children, and we had a baby. But to hell with the village, bugger the village and the whole district. But I won't say a word, I'll shut up,' – here she started to laugh – 'because the way his daddy used to chirp at him like a bird, he could have been a peacock or a swan.'

She wiped her nose on a kitchen cloth and poured us both another glass.

'My parents had my brother when they were in their forties too, so what?' I say 'He's more normal than many others, my dear, Gale is. Nightingale is a real artist, that thing with the letters to his neighbours, that's in fact a great performance.' I wanted to say something consoling. 'Besides, Gale and I are similar, nonsensical, a bad lot here. Each to his own.'

'You're an artist, for sure, how come he is? He scribbles on walls, upsets people. The police are after him.' She chomped on her carob, which must have been too hard, because she spat it out into the sink. 'If he's so clever, why's he skint?'

She was angry, her cheeks flushed.

'Is there a performance where he doesn't get in touch with his mother for a year and more? Or makes a child he doesn't even know exists for two years,' she adds.

'That's bit radical.' (Does Gale have a child?)

'Radical, radical.' She agreed.

Then she changed the subject; she ran through the TV programmes and politics and made us supper after which I kicked off my high heels, washed in completely cold water, because there was no hot water in the boiler, and quickly fell asleep in Gale's childhood bed in the white room.

Beside the pillow, on a little table, lay a mouth organ, polished, cheerful, and beside the bed was a pair of school slippers, size 10. I had never seen such enormous school slippers, a child's object. Josipa had left them out for me, but they were several sizes too big. There were a few school readers on the shelves, in the drawers neatly folded clothes belonging to some former child who would never return. The boat's log-book, which I am looking for, is almost certainly not there, the old lady would have found it already. They never got on, the controversial Nightingale and his old mother.

Above the bed hung a tapestry of the Mona Lisa, which had once been sewn long ago by the young Josipa. The village women thought it was the Holy Virgin, she told me, smiling, 'let them think so, let them, bugger me if I care what they think!'

For years afterwards the embroidered Mona Lisa became an important figure in Gale's stories, sonnets, sketches and strip-cartoons. In the room, it rests calmly in the whiteness of the empty walls behind glass in an ornate plaster frame, sometimes friendly and gentle, but sometimes capricious and caustic, the Gioconda pricked out 13,190 times with a needle.

'I don't get that, what's the point of these tapestries, who dreamed them up, what a scandalous waste of time. Is it obtuse or Zen? That's crap, it's really like my work. Except – I do it for money.'

That thought used to warm me like hot sun, but with time, with time it has cooled down a lot. But, hey, let's get back to the story.

Around seven in the morning, we opened, then closed, the house door. I set off towards the car, accompanied by Josipa. She had a new headscarf, yellow, with blue peonies, non-existent in nature, but nevertheless peonies, wonderful peonies.

'You're dead set on finding him … Watch out for the *mujahideen*!'

I started the car.

'Why them?'

'They were on the News yesterday.'

'Don't believe the News, my dear.'

Perhaps it isn't fair to tell an old person not to believe the News, that might freak them out, I thought. But still, I probably don't have much clue about old people, my parents aren't alive (my Ma died three years ago, darling). I remembered them beautiful, in their prime – they didn't have a chance to get on my nerves. A friend of mine said that old people have selective deafness and they only take in what they want or can bear to hear.

Josipa shouted: 'I'm only joking, I'm joking!'

I felt better, although I would not have sworn blind that she really was joking. I didn't want to think of Josipa as a bigoted old hag, it's hard to love people, they often mess things up. It would be nicer if dear, kind people weren't chauvinistic idiots, but they are. I got out of the car quickly and hugged her, tight. 'We'll be in touch!'

I see her in my head (I do see her, now, clearly). A tall old lady, the tallest among the babushkas. The mother of my former seasonal bridegroom – the unrecovered-from Nightingale – is waving to me with both hands. It's an Indian summer and in that pose she could be a mascot for it. Above her flowery head goldfinches flitted into the empty, pale early-morning sky, and the clock on the old bell-tower, the one I already mentioned, was still showing three in the afternoon.

I set off towards the border, towards Bosnia. The road swallowed me sullenly.

All right, I'll tell you. So, my name is Clementine. On the outside, I'm a blonde orange. I have silicon lips, I have a Brazilian hairstyle, I drive a two-seater Mazda MX-5 convertible, gold, but inside I'm a black orange. Full of black juice.

The day before my meeting with Nightingale's mother, the meeting with which I began this story, I travelled from Ljubljana to Split. I decided to make the journey after I had spent the whole of the preceding week vainly calling Gale every day. When I tried to pay money for the boat's berth I discovered that his account had been closed months before, at the marina they told me he had paid all his bills, but, they'd noticed that for some time no one had been coming to the boat. His mobile was dead and at first that annoyed me, then it worried me (we had not been in touch often, in fact very rarely in recent years, and then mainly in connection with our shared boat, but nevertheless).

Then I began calling his family, our common acquaintances, our former neighbours: a whole lost life so unconnected with my present life that it could have been anyone's, and that whole mini-Atlantis rose to the surface, my dear. None of the people Gale and I had known could say exactly in which direction that sexy bird had flown off last summer. They weren't troubled, not even his mother to whom he had simply mentioned that he had something to do in Bosnia, not even she was troubled, she just looked anxious for a moment, or so it seemed to me, because that crazy Gale came and went like that, no one ever knew when. What I found on the Internet turned out to be of most use: the blog he had written for a while had been dead for a long time, he had completely abandoned the virtual life which he had in any case found vulgar, but Google knew anyway – he had worked for a while in Libya, then in Chernobyl. Then a photograph appeared and was published on a foreign portal: a mural with Bosnia and his name written under it. And that was all.

Officially, he lived in our old street, Dinko Šimunović Street, on the tenth floor in the same building and flat in which I had spent some time with him, but, as I said, I knew nothing about the last years of his life, although in the depths of my heart he had remained my beloved. It's not that other loves hadn't come along, my dear, but in Gale's case that had no bearing on my preference.

My encounter with Dinko Šimunović Street two weeks earlier had not been agreeable (had so many years really passed?). I stepped into the street cautiously and briskly, not looking around too much. It was a hot afternoon and the street was deserted, although little stars beside the intercom indicated that tourists had penetrated even into these concrete oases. Gale is right, it's the loveliest street in Split, a serious street, not a little street, lovely little streets are something else, there are lots of them, but I like big streets. And I like tall buildings and skyscrapers. And I like the twentieth century more than the nineteenth or the seventh. I'm not sure about the twenty-first yet. I once lived here as a child, with my parents, but, after my father died, my mother and brother moved to a smaller town and sold our flat (every inaccessible dirty join, every hidden crack was mine), I moved just a few hundred metres east, to Gale's place (Ma could never forgive me, poor Ma, I left her so easily).

I don't know which was worse in my encounter with Šimunović Street: what had stayed the same or what had changed. I didn't have the time or the will for such emotions, to stop and rethink. I hadn't expected it to shake me up. It was like that situation when you rush out in your slippers to empty the rubbish and meet some shithead from your childhood who keeps you standing beside the dustbin for fifteen minutes and under his insistent gaze you grow visibly older and more decrepit, fatter. The street looked at me, it watched me patiently, from all directions. I had to look at it, in passing, to see where I was walking: skyscrapers, tall, slender buildings, the flight of steps, the sea. This was a return to the intimate, oh boy.

The things we have and know drain away and vanish, new ones cover them over like grass over a grave; the world of the inert is closest to death. If anyone thinks I'm mistaken, let them try to imagine a town without birds, insects or people, a town of inanimate things.

Or a hill without plants.

Or an old dance hall filled with the ghosts of dancers.

Or a house through which war has swirled, after which the blood has congealed and it has been aired of the stench of soldiers' boots, the hot, sweaty grenades have cooled and lie in wait, put away in the bottom of a cupboard, tucked under bedding.

Or a snowy wasteland when the sun goes down behind a mountain.

Or a closed road.

A factory: machines and turbines without workers.

That is emptiness such as a real desert will never know, because for centuries nothing has inhabited it apart from eternity. It is not unusual for people to imagine the setting of paradise just like that. At that moment there is more death in a cup after the coffee has been drunk and the colour drained, than in the Sahara.

Gale (I'm always debating with him in my head) believed in technological progress in the spirit of socialism and used to say that at some stage soon, when people, all people, would be going on outings to the Moon, he would put on an exhibition there of all the things that are important, to everyone, or at least to him. There's no atmosphere there, no oxidation, and so no death of the inert and objects we care about really will last forever or at least longer than us. He would reproduce the whole of our street. Of course, when you're seventeen, it's easy to fall in love with someone who wants to put on an exhibition on the Moon in order to save beautiful or important things from decay, although I was already aware then that if not everyone could go to Tito's island of Brioni, they wouldn't get to the Moon either.

And what's left for death if you forget everything before it? Is there anything left to die? When things turn the wrong way round and oblivion precedes death instead of death oblivion? It's presumably a defence mechanism if the body decays so rapidly after it's emptied by oblivion.

Where were we? Oh yes, Šimunović Street. Proof that tall buildings and skyscrapers can be attractive, that third Split, Split 3, Trstenik, my borough. Proof that socialism can be beautiful, as Gale would say.

In the lift, opposite the door to the flat, I straightened my skirt and fixed my make-up. Without lipstick a woman is naked, my mother used to say and that habit of using make-up, which some people find stupid, but is definitely entertaining, has remained with me from my teens.

'Stone ve crows. I mus' be dreamin',' that's what the man in his thirties who introduced himself as Joe Pironi said when he opened the door, with a smile. He was wearing Bermudas: between his thin hairy legs a Maltese (called Corto, wittily but really) peered and barked at me. The next thing I noticed about Pironi was his oversized shaved head and blue eyes with half-closed lids.

'Is someone, like, makin' a film?' Here he paused and lit a cigarette. 'I know, crap joke.'

I stood on the threshold genuinely afraid of the dog's snarling little teeth and explained that I was looking for Gale. I said I hadn't seen him in years, maybe ten, but I wanted to sell the boat, quickly, and I needed his agreement. The boat was in his name, my dear, but it was still my boat, my inheritance, although, it's true, he had maintained it the whole time. I scowl when I lie, but no matter, Pironi wasn't listening to me in any case.

He said: 'Who'd ever fink, mate. You wouldn' credit it! So it never crossed 'is daft mind vat he knows you and you'd come for the keys of the boat. Yeah, the cunt knew you'd come. You and Gale, man and wife, good as. But 'e's not 'ere, ol' girl. He went off to look for someone he made a kid wiv two or free years ago. He may be in Bosnia – Livno or Tuzla – or Timbuctoo. If you ask me, it's not worth lookin'. Better wait till 'e gets in touch.'

The Malteser in Pironi's arms was still barking. He put it down on a table and from a drawer took out cigarette papers, tobacco and grass. The little dog spun round in a circle and tried to get down. I didn't have time to wait for him (Gale) to get in touch. There were no books on the shelves, not a single one, which meant he had no intention of coming back. But still, his strange writing outfit was dangling from a hanger on the door of the wardrobe as though he had left it there the previous day.

Pironi said: 'Wan' a puff? Since you're 'ere, we could spark up a bit? 'S no fun solo. Homegrown, from Vis, not sprayed, sweet as honey.'

'What the hell,' I said, 'it must be healthy, I'll have a drag.'

We sprawled on the couch. Corto retreated under it and curled up between our shoes.

Pironi said: 'Struth, ol' girl, I wouldn' con you for ve world, I've no clue where that waster's buggered off to, maybe Travnik, maybe Bugojno. I'm just, like, looking after the flat. You know, a Croat, so's it's occupied, if you get my drift. Last summer, before he scarpered, he got up the nose of the whole neighbourhood, the police were after him, you wouldn' believe it. Vat made him mad, he didn't expect that kind of reaction to his letters. It's unreal, you know, 'e's a dreamer. I told him – give it a rest, bro, forget those jerks, mind your own business.'

I said that, in actual fact, it was Gale's business. 'He's an artist, my dear, he has to interact with his surroundings, he has to change them.'

'You're kidding me, yeah? I'm an artist too. You must've seen those graffiti: *I'm hungry, give me what you can*, in front of the door, above the intercom? Right, you saw it. I'm not pretentious like some vat puts on an act, I'm more interested in reality.'

I asked him whether he was a gay activist, because it looked to me like gay graffiti although it had a socio-economic base. He asked, of course, did I want to find out and laughed: 'how did I know it didn't mean give me salami in my sandwich, for instance?'

'You've got a dirty little mind,' he said, grinning.

He said, Pironi did, that Gale had nearly got him in the shit with those letters, and something else about some business with explosives placed in a Split bank, because on the wall people had found the same sentences as in one of Gale's letters. 'They had him in, for questioning, twice,' said Pironi, 'but they couldn't pin anything on him, because the letters had been sent to the whole street, several hundred copies.' (Magnificent, magnificent)

But nothing concrete about where I might find Gale.

Last summer, the June before last, somewhat more than a year ago, in Dinko Šimunović Street some unknown lovers had made love loudly until dawn, waking the sleeping populace, and it was a hot summer, with daytime temperatures of forty-two and airless nights and many wide open windows.

Judging by everything Joe Pironi told me, and he told me a lot, disjointedly, I gathered the following: the letters that Gale had zeal-ously dropped into his neighbours' mailboxes had upset the whole street. They upset the street more than the reason they were written, although that too had sent sparks flying. I was agreeably surprised by their lack of indifference, even if it was negative. I was used to people here reacting only to football, which made Gale think them limited and worthy of contempt, but I was more tolerant and practical, because these were the people we had grown up with, I would have felt oppressed to think negatively about them or to think about them at all. Compromise, always compromise, well, I had to live with people or die alone.

In June of last year in Dinko Šimunović Street, Gale worked by night, so Joe Pironi told me: a well-known foreign, American, magazine had commissioned a strip cartoon from him, which was important to him – I presume it still is important to him – and noise interfered with his concentration.

On the tenth evening he, Gale, not Pironi, felt a powerful moral obligation to ask the overly-loud lovers to be a bit quieter (I don't really believe that). But since, according to Pironi, he didn't know who the moaners were, he wrote to almost everyone, working his way systematically, scattering letters into their letterboxes, but the groaning continued for three whole weeks, maybe even longer, into the second week of July. The street has this unusual cascading architecture, narrow buildings with hundreds of windows, and if someone is making love by the south-facing windows, high under the clouds, it is no simple matter to determine the source. It lasted for three whole weeks, maybe even longer, into the second week of July. Then it stopped.

And before Nightingale completed his game with the letters, which he had evidently entered into with his whole comical, idiotic and wonderful soul, a meeting of the tenants' councils of the buildings nearest to the sighing in Šimunović Street was called:

the letters were collected and handed over to the police:

the police didn't really know what to do with the material,

they warned Gale that he was causing a disturbance, threatening him with reporting him for violating the peace and public order,

'Crazy stuff,' said Pironi.

In short, as far as I could make out, they banned him from completing his 'project' of letters to the neighbourhood.

'Banned him? What was craziest of all,' said Pironi, 'vey even accused 'im that 'e, Gale, was ve maniac groaning in ve night.'

Pironi didn't believe that (nor do I), but he couldn't confirm it, as he was at that time living with another friend in another part of town.

Pironi said: 'What do vey mean 'project', honeybun, 'e calls it artistic expression when 'e takes a piss. Get it, it's a question of morals how far you as an artist should invade people's privacy. On ve other 'and you keep invading it, ven it's a question of packaging, if you get my drift. You 'as to package it, mate, I say, but he doesn't listen.'

'He didn't package it – that's the problem,' I say.

'And did they discover who it was? Who was the doer of the debauchery?'

They didn't, they never did, they calmed down. But it was madness, his bicycle had once broken down so he spent the night at Gale's place while it was going on. 'It wasn't true,' he said. 'You see what this street is like, a million open windows, it reverberates: it could have been anyone.' (It's unseemly for people to go around at night banging on doors to check whether folk are fucking.)

Gale's flat/bed-sitter stretched around me – I was looking for windows – a rather large room with no internal walls, different from the flat I remember, which did not seem to suit the Gale I had known, and that lack of recognition disheartened me (and maybe frightened me).

I said to Pironi: ' What kind of morals, don't make me laugh. Someone's letters really bug them. Matey.'

He said: 'Hey, ol' girl, take it easy, you're gettin' het up for nothing. I haven' a clue what he wrote to 'em, but it got to 'em. You can ask Bogdan Diklić to show you the letters. He's on the first floor. He's not an actor, no way. Chair of the Tenants' Council, that type. Shall I go? D'you fink I've got more chance with Bogdan Diklić than you?! Why, you're a celebrity! You'd feel awkward. Ah, ha, so you're not that famous. I get you, but there's no fuckin' way Diklić will give me ve letters. He takes it seriously. I mean seriously seriously. He's fifty and he lives wiv 'is mother, 'e doesn't even jerk off any more, 'e 'as to take fings seriously. Chair of the Tenants' Council. Another smoke? Ok, ol' girl, all ve more for me.'

Something along those lines. As he talked, Pironi's verbal ping-pong balls skittered round about, bouncing off the rubber edges of my consciousness. After a while I became aware of an agreeable warmth on my feet.

Pironi yelled: 'Corto, son of a bitch! Hey, ol' girl, don't be mad, ol' girl. You're 'is now, 'e's marked you, now he finks you're, you know, okay.'

Like hell.

I wasn't angry. Joe Pironi went to the toilet to get a sponge and paper to wipe up the dog's pee, but since he was taking his time, I used paper handkerchiefs and water from the kitchen tap. In passing, strategically, I opened a few drawers where Gale's things ought to have been, in case I could somewhere catch sight of the boat's log, but they were empty. I stuffed his writing outfit into my bag, deciding I had a right to it (as his former wife, my dear, I could always try that line). Corto followed me with his little pink tongue out. Unlike big dogs, which filled me with confidence, I've always been afraid of small dogs as of all other hysterics … I wagged my finger at him, opened the door, summoned the lift. Although it was the ground floor.

Maybe I could have knocked on Diklić's door on the first floor, but I didn't feel like it. I was a bit high, peed-on, sweaty and hungry and not in a very good mood, and the chances of some zealous chair of the tenants' council passing those incriminating letters over to me were, even without all the aforementioned, minimal. (What madness, who on earth would run away because of a bunch of letters.)

On my way out, at the lobby door, I came across two thin little girls playing with a plastic doll. 'I'm not sure I love you,' one of them told the doll seriously and crossly, and then hid it from me. No one in the street, midday scorching heat, the town is still full of tourists at this time, down in the necropolis, in the centre, on the beaches, but Split district 3 is wonderfully empty as though the whole summer had lain down over it to rest a bit.

My eye was caught by a grafitto on the flyover under which one could see the sea and on which someone had written in huge letters MEANING. In the distance I heard the honk of a ferry horn, the captain's intrepid bass baritone. Oh Nightingale, where on earth are you? Where've you been my whole life?

Before dusk fell, I went to the marina, to Woody Mary, our boat.

She was swaying in the dark shallows of the harbour, bewitching as ever, at least to me.

She was in the same place, at the same jetty, as before, but unlike his flat, Gale did take care of the boat: freshly painted, white and blue as in the song, brass and copper gleaming, polished, although a year had passed, and more, since the captain's departure, and the boat's teak – rosy, warm-blooded, and alive beneath my hand, and, seeing that there was no one near, I kissed it loudly.

I hugged the good, constant, beloved Woody Mary like I used to, when I would throw myself down on the prow, carefree, wet and happy, like a young bitch.

I sat on the stern for a while, airing my head.

A light mistral breeze towards evening and a pink sky promising fine weather in the west. If I were to photograph or describe that scene it would be banal kitsch. Beautiful things have no need of art, which has already long been better suited to the half ugly or entirely vile.

A producer once flattered me: that's why people like your series, good-looking lovers, emotions, falling in love, happy end, all that life denies them and that contemporary art cannot give them. That's how one producer flattered me (not Kalemengo, Kalemengo is a decent guy), but one who wanted to have it off with me, in which in the end he succeeded, probably because at that stage of my life I was denied all of the above: good-looking lovers, emotions, falling in love among other things.

And to make matters worse, that poor dreary slob of a producer who produces productions was right.

People needed a lot of cheap, quick emotion, they needed it in greater quantities than it was possible to produce, teams of typists banged away on keyboards, churning out total nebulousness, without investing an iota of passion in it, just angry typing slaves' sweat, but out of that sweat germinated and bloomed abundant, copious magnificent gunk which in turn generated laughter and tears, loves, fears and passions and moved people like the best works of art.

Let's face it, gunk has moved the vast majority of people and filled their thoughts probably more than the best work of art ever could.

Oh no: oh yes. That's the way it is.

At the end of that day, my mobile showed twenty-four unanswered calls (a dozen from Kalemengo, two from my brother, and – to my surprise – two from Bert), but not one I felt like replying to. When it rang again, I wondered how it would be to throw the phone into the sea and watch it sink, dumb and deaf. It would be like a small victory. However, that momentary relief would have brought existential complications, and I had already decided to return to Ljubljana as soon as day broke. So instead I switched the mobile off until morning (sleep, sleep little master).

When I finally unlocked the door of the boat, moved aside the hatch cover and slipped under the prow where I was to spend the first night of the journey I am writing about, things changed: Although I rummaged through everything, I didn't find the boat's log in the boat either, but under the mast, on the table, carefully laid in a box, those letters of Gale's awaited me (I shall read some of them here).

The difference between Gale and a lunatic lies in the fact that Gale is a worker, truly Japanese in his craft. Had he engaged in any slightly more lucrative occupation with as much zeal, who knows, my dear, he would be a wealthy man. So, I crawled in under the prow and read until my torch battery gave out – since I didn't have a clue where the electricity cable was.

LETTER FROM A WISTFUL DOG

Distinguished people, canine friends and others,

I believe you are familiar with the little acoustic scandal that has been rocking our neighbourhood in recent days, or perhaps you are the very ones who have been filling our silent nights with decibels of passion – whatever.

Whether you make love quietly like dogs or loudly like cats is not the main issue, I am addressing you with the desire, prompted by the aforementioned events, to share with you a dog's thoughts about love. In this appeal, I ask just one thing of you: that, caught up in a vortex of passion or exasperated or astounded by feverish cries from the darkness, you do not forget that as well as feline love that screeches there is also canine love that whines. Remember that at least in the morning, when the common sense and innocence of a beginning briefly reign, toss a bone or two to those genuinely hungry for love and meat.

This letter is also a study of unrequited loyalty – it is well-known that loyalty is inherent in canine love. But loyalty, contrary to widespread and superficial conviction, is not always monogamous, just as monogamy need not always be loyal or devoted, with either humans or dogs.

You may remember, perhaps, the handsome mixture of schnauzer and who-knows-what dog from our street, whom you called Shakespeare-in-love? That shaggy fellow (we'll go on calling him Shakespeare, so there's no confusion), at the time of the banishment of a certain little bitch Gara from the district of Mertojak, would run away from his comfortable home in Šimunović Street, to settle himself outside her gate. For three years in a row, he exposed himself to peril by dashing through the busy streets, for two weeks he would be without a roof over his head, hungry and thirsty, dependent on charity; he sat outside her courtyard resolutely, like a hairy monument, waiting for Gara to show her little tail.

Barking intrepidly and baring her teeth, she drove all other dogs from her hindquarters, which was not easy, because, we all remember, when her mistress took her out for walks, she would return at a run, with her little dog in her arms, accompanied by insatiable Alsatians, Labradors and Dachshunds which had broken their chains and, driven by their senses, roamed through the streets wordlessly and furiously pleading for a partner.

But only one, outside that hypnotised pack, made a suitable mate for her and as soon as her mistress looked away, little Gara would leap over the fence, lift up her tail, and Shakespeare-in-love would readily lock on.

Once, when they were locked like that, blinded like an amorous Janus, the unfortunate happy couple spent hours outside the back entrance to the building, and your children tugged at them and threw stones at them – but they were unable to part. That can even happen to humans, sometimes a timorous heart can block the nether regions, let alone to dogs whose brains are full of moonlight and adrenalin.

When, for the second spring in a row, Gara's young mistress was surprised by a damp heap of puppies in her laundry basket, that marked the end of Gara and Shakespeare-in-love's romantic liaison.

After the procedure, Gara was no longer up for anything, uninterested in mating, she gave herself up to food and melancholy, while Shakespeare transferred his amorous vigil a few streets further away to Luna the spaniel and remained hers faithfully for ever more.

After Luna came Hani the pug. His affair with the pug resulted in some interesting offspring of the canine genus, and, consequentially, the dog's master reined him in, so that he was no longer seen without a leash, starry-eyed and frisky.

But before and after these serial monogamies, canine erotic romances, golden ringlets and defiant bristles, excavated bones and painful balls, Shakespeare always returned to his human. The dog did not resent it even when he had him castrated. Indeed, it focused his faithfulness and he was in a way grateful that he had been freed from sexual tension. Now he was able to adore his dear human friend with his whole being, with the unconditional, unrestrained, platonic, mad and pure love that only dogs bestow. His unalloyed devotion did not end even when his man abandoned him, leaving him in the street, why yes, like a cur, as people rightly say.

Only a dog can have such a stupid heart. A dog like me, a religious fanatic.

You know me? Shakespeare-in-love, the tailless ragamuffin, from a Schnauzer mother and unidentified terrier. Maybe you yelled at me when I was rolling a beef bone I'd stolen from the butcher down the street, maybe you kicked a stone in my direction or threw a bunch of keys at me when I sniffed your coiffured pup's backside.

Towards the end of spring, my best friend left me in the wood beside the slaughterhouse, over there by the motorway, I walked for seven nights and six days, got home, with a bloody nose and torn paws and in the morning, in front of his house, when he was leaving for work, I threw myself at his feet, crazy with joy. He stopped in surprise and then said: scram!

And that was all.

I still wait for him in the morning, outside the building. I don't throw myself at his feet, I stand to one side and wait, I only whine when he has gone.

Neither dirt nor poverty have dimmed the shine of my humiliation. Is there anything more dignified than being humiliated in love? It is a spectacular fall and the further you fall, the deeper is your sorrow, and the more magnificent your pain. You who skirt around me in the street, fearful and disgusted, should know that whenever you kick me you send me to the sky, along with your contempt, my love-luff-uff-uff that no one needs becomes ever more beautiful, this suffering could make a holy dog of me.

I've seen this too: a few days ago, my human bought a new dog. I don't despair and I don't hope, but I still wait. Besides, where could I go with this invisible chain with which I was born.

So, I ask you again, because I am a scrounger and beggar and skinflint if necessary – caught up in the vortex of passion or exasperated or astounded by feverish cries from the darkness, do not forget that in addition to feline love that screeches, there is also canine love that whines. Remember that at least in the morning, when the goodwill of a beginning briefly reigns, toss at least a bone to those genuinely hungry for the meat of hope.

Yours faithfully,
A Wistful Dog

If I had to describe Nightingale in two words, I'd say he is a street poet.

Although since he was twenty-something when he published a *samizdat* edition of just ten poems, he hasn't written any poems but everything he has done could be called poetry. His collection was even called *Poetry*, which is neither good nor bad, but simply accurate. They were interesting poems, authentic, but he felt that he needed a new means of expression, for him paper was slow, dull and uncommunicative, while the Internet is garrulous, polluted and cacophonous, those are places that don't offer space for development, that's what he thought. He wrote poems with a felt-tip on walls, by night, on peeling façades, in lifts, toilets, on rubbish skips, in subways. He drew. He discovered spray paint. An excellent concept, always fashionable, he liked spray.

He said that when the poets left the streets, it was a bad day for poetry.
Because the first poets were guttersnipes;
noble Homeroid beggars,
the occasional Villon beyond the law,
Byrons who typically limp on the other side of the law,
and beatniks,
their distant relatives Cendrarses,
whole brigades of Bukowskys,
a few Bolans,
Rimbauds, Wildes, Verlaines, Dalmatian reporters,

          rappers …
gentle decadents, anonymous painters and grafitti writers, Banksy
          et al,

and too few women, poets,
(maybe, if we stretch the term, Tracy Emin? Nin, Anaïs?)
because for too long over the centuries their wanderings
have been hampered by the skirts and children round their legs.
The threshold of the house
and men's shoes
women's too, pointed.
On the other side of the street music wafts
from rhapsodes, troubadours, cantators, street singers:
young backpackers with a guitar.
They were all his gambling fathers and prostituted brothers,
although, although,
he used to say
you never know whose dad is whose.

Gale said that the poets were ruined when they focused on each other and their medium, language, and stopped thinking about the people they were addressing. They perfected their tools, they precisely tuned their instruments, but they sang into emptiness, with empty words, and empty space responded.

But bollocks to the poets and pseudo-poets, they will always have poetry, the blessed idiots.

Nevertheless, the first thing I heard about Nightingale was not that he was a poet or a grafitti artist, comic-strip maker or art student, and he was all of that, but that he was visited by women, all sorts of women and girls, when they fancied sex, unpaid of course, for he was not a tart. Approachable and affable, he would say: benign.

It was all strange to me, because at the time I kept seeing him with a girl, whom we called Helanka, she was a refugee from Bosnia, better known as a girl without a single hair (about which she gave various explanations). At that time I didn't know there could be male/female friendships, because we had been taught they didn't exist. And I didn't know that Gale, Helanka and I would become inseparable for that brief phase of youth when your friends are more important than anything and anyone, but that passes as though it had never been, hello-goodbye, each to his own path forever and no matter.

A village, a melancholy village. Why is a village more alarming than a town? The smallest village is more alarming than the biggest town, isn't it? No one locks their door for fear of burglars, but before long here comes your next-door neighbour tapping on the door with an axe. I'm not a fan of villages.

But what can you do, the heart does not ask, after I had left the village of Mitrovići behind me, on my search for Gale, I set out towards the village of Tulumbe in pursuit of my Helanka, because wherever she was he could have been too.

Tulumbe is a village of ghosts, on a mountain between clumps of hazel and meadows full of blueberries. The old Red School in the middle of the fields is concealed by wild corn, and the long burned-out houses have been taken over by plants. Here and there the occasional light in the darkness, a lantern, a generator humming, electricity never reached here, nor asphalt, nor mains water, but there is that delicious water from the forest well, and if the well dries up, there are springs in the villages down the hill. I heard all that, all that and more, my dear, some time ago, and soon I would see for myself. That was two weeks ago, a little less, at the start of my search, at the sweet start, and it was sweet, I can see that now...

I drove tirelessly across and beyond the border, deep into the deserted land of Bosnia, through glistening red and black forests and through canyons full of wild beasts' eyes, through gigantic greens, a moist tearful landscape of magnanimous beauty and past the peeling façades of towns.

Every minaret and every gilded church bell-tower, and they were as numerous as house chimneys, reminded me of an evil phallus.

Evil phalluses are always ready to thrust. 'Oh God, wherever you may be!' my grandmother used to say as she watched devastation on television or when she spilled coffee on the tablecloth. If he exists and if he's worth his salt, of one thing I am certain: from the outset he avoids places of worship.

I drove, without a break, from dawn to dusk, along little by-ways that don't exist on Sat-Nav, I got lost and then found myself, evening caught me on a road with not one single lit window and the blood in my veins had frozen repeatedly.

And then I became accustomed to the east, studded with tiny stars. The night was not yet impenetrable – soon a small town in a hollow would be revealed by the headlights and beyond it was the village I was looking for. I did not stop until I reached my goal. Such a journey ought perhaps, no, certainly, to be planned, more things and warmer clothes brought along, a different car, not to attract attention, but I had not had time for plans. Freed from plans, from responsibility, from obligations. (I am alone and therefore free, says the optimist. My dear. I am free and therefore alone, says the pessimist.)

If anyone saw me at the one traffic light or at the queue at the border, he would look round questioningly, one person even shouted: 'Hey, there's Clementine, the blond, the soap girl!'

I have silicon lips and perfectly whitened teeth, I have a Brazilian hairstyle, soft and expensive, if crumpled, clothes, I drive a gold Mazda convertible, but I am a black orange, inside. Full of hell.

I'm going to a melancholy village. The road devours me sullenly, but the night – the night is glad of me.

LETTER FROM AN INDIFFERENT GOD

Who's this waking me?

I'm an old, tired God and I have to sleep, because I have to calculate, I have to arrange things, I have to do book-keeping, I have to write down everything that has come in and out of my mouth, I have to digest it all, I have to empty all those inboxes of prayers. Day and night, I sit bowed over the Earth, sorting: a prayer for health, a prayer for forgiveness, a prayer for success, a prayer for a life, but sometimes also a prayer for death. I do my work in a professional manner, the profession of God, I don't delve into the meaning.

Well, hey, what else could I do; you're so pathetic, so feeble: blind puppies looking for their mummy, little children for whom their father assumes responsibility. You don't need a God, just a prosperous parent! An illusionist! A fortune-teller and lottery-drum, that's the ideal God for you.

Who's waking me with their sighs?

I'm a God in your image, a conformist God, an indifferent God, a God who doesn't lose His head, and has forgotten how to fall in love, that was so long ago. When I fall in love, when I feel my body, I who am incorporeal, become a frenzied rapist, a sodomiser and pornographer god, a GHB god and drink-spiker who attacks women and boys disguised as an animal or a spirit, and men disguised as fire or a knife. I'm Achilles and Jesus's daddy, and, allegedly also the Cyclops, they're all my pitiful, slain bastards.

It's true, my love is thieving, criminal, out of control – you would say blasphemous.

But I gave you that signal, finely tuned, the best of myself, a divine spark, a little gift. And what did you do with it? What does love mean to you? Did you love? You faint-hearted folk who have never felt a divine surge of the blood, you have reduced my gift to your narrow measure, you took fright: first for centuries you forbade others from loving, now you forbid it for yourselves.

While I, let me say it again, it's a well-known fact, I am nothing other than you, your image, your prototype: if you are in love and I am the God of epiphany, your amorous sighs and your laughter are praise for me, I can hardly bear your psychopathic sufferings, hysterical sacrifices, hatreds, prayers and restraint.

I am God, creator, author! I am not a supernatural being produced in the sterile conditions of church laboratories – I am dithyramb, firework, holy heathen. The millennia were hard and repellent, but also full of inspiration for a young god, sprung from wine, dance, thunder, from thought, from a burst star, from the sun, no less! God is immoderate in love, whether he has a form or the face of a totem, a demented saint, an epileptic or wild goddess.

Whoever is waking me, is waking me at a bad moment in the century just begun which I had awaited for a long time with a trembling heart, like a lover who promised tenderness and delights, understanding and harmony, but turned out violent and obtuse.

Let them leave me to carry out my judicial tasks in the indifference which you assigned me, I have found peace here, a flat desk on which I sort out these innumerable prayers.

Should I refer to your merchant priests? Should the likes of them be my PR? Hatred is the only heresy, but indifference is worse. And here too is the hypocrisy of their golden chalices and vestments. What have they to do with the divine? A cross to cross me out with. Could a God, a creator, an artist of genius, be enthused by the dryness of bishops' underwear and dribbling lips that preach fear and ignorance?

Why, from my finger sprang the mango, the peacock's tail, Sophia Loren. From the clicking of my tongue fell all the languages of the world, first the tongues of Africa, then the others, including the song of birds and the laughter of small babies.

So sumptuous, mighty and tender can I be.

I no longer wish to have anything to do with scoundrels, I'm too old for such crap. I'm waiting to retire and stick seals on your uneasy consciences.

At some stage I want to be everyone's God. A magnanimous, powerful and comical father. Until then – make your own way,

Amen.

The sea is more beautiful than cathedrals. But are rivers more beautiful than lively town streets or are streets sometimes more beautiful than rivers and streams? Some Saturday, any morning of that spring, the streets down which I made my way to the sea were lovelier than waterfalls. Full of sky, flowers, fountains and birds, full of people in sunglasses, thin t-shirts and linen trousers. My eyes were seventeen years old and all of that was spread out in front of them in bright shades as I stepped towards the *Valley of the First Menstruation*.

Today (twenty years ago), Marko and Bert are waiting for me there. They've parked their Vespas by St Franjo's and occupied their patch. They are knights with plastic helmets, the small rulers of our hearts. In honour of them, and many other boys before and after them who were the object of collective adoration for a brief flash of youth, on that patch the *Valley of the First Menstruation* was formed, it was where secondary schoolgirls used to hang out – although the term is inaccurate and behind the times and generally gave rise to disapproval, it imposed itself tacitly. After the schoolgirls came guys, they put gel in their hair and their hands in their pockets. When Marko and Bert and their Vespas change their patch in a year's time, the whole Valley will move after them to a new place, first the girls, and then the boys with them.

Great care is taken not to cross the border between the Valley of the FM and the Outland, where the yokels are, although no one strives for a different status here, on the Quay. The yokels don't give a damn about being yokels, they are in the majority and they have a good time. Besides, soon, as soon as they mature, even the little fashionable girls will leave the little phonies Marko and

Bert and their bikes and climb into the yokels' well-groomed cars. They will like their little gold chains, their loud yokel music, thin tank-tops on body-built torsos, sneakers and minimalist trainers, their marble and brass interiors. There were days when I regretted that I wasn't a real pure-bred yokel, that their whole culture didn't bore me, that I genuinely enjoyed folk-songs, rave and techno, that I liked everything associated with that: clubs where you party till dawn, they were the only ones who felt truly good in this country, they were the only ones who enjoyed themselves, while everyone else lazed about, they had somewhere to go where there was always some dosh around, there was whisky, cola, macchiato, free entry to the club, coke snorted from new big banknotes. It's more or less the same now. At times I wanted to live in a bare plastered house with three floors, with no plumbing, unencumbered, with a crazy car in the yard and a t-shirt with Versace emblazoned on it, not to worry about anything other than my false nails falling off, but here's the problem: I'm a girl and along with that story goes a guy who would have sometimes given me a punch with his fist or at least a slap, who would make me kids and imprison me at home between two masses, and I would no longer enjoy being a pure-bred yokel. There's no country where life's good for a yokel girl, only for yokel lads.

Today (twenty years ago) everyone is on the Quay and the Quay is everything. This is the first sun after the winter and everyone avoids staying inside the town walls – the best cafés inside the walls are run by dykes, they hang together and get each other jobs – that's the theory. They've found some way of coping with the half-people involved in protection rackets round the cafés. They are the only ones who can do that, survive, and they are probably used to everything in order to subsist, so thought Helanka, my friend who knew everything. (Everyone was a bit crazy for her and her freedom, and she also had an appearance that opened the doors of the marginalised and marginal groups to her.)

The folk who go to the dykes in bad weather, are today (twenty years ago) sitting north-east of Outland, because that's the Valley of the Geeks, that's where coffee is drunk by the nonchalant intelligentsia, with a few young alternatives tagging along, every town has its snobs, but here they are probably the best people the town has, at least that's what they believe; only you have to observe them individually, yes, individually, never together, if you don't want your heart to shrink to extra small. It's not too much, it's not even a lot, but everything is prettified on that postcard. No one is going to stumble into the wrong valley or sit on the wrong chair, if he does not wish to sit alone.

Only the mega-yokel Nightingale in camouflage pants imposes himself on everyone, the moron, but he gets on my nerves particularly when he sits beside us secondary schoolgirls. 'You go to Matejuško's, to the drunks, you acid head, to the Little Boss and co., you'll fit in,' says a girl yesterday (twenty years ago), but some people laugh at him, he's funny, he has nice eyes. Nothing offends him, nothing.

The war is over, the war is near its end, that's already clear. Someone ought to tell him that the war is nearly over and that he shouldn't wear those camouflage pants any more. It's Saturday, there's no school, there's not even any war. Let him first have a wash and a haircut, and then let him come among us, we're young and attractive, who cares if we have only one pair of denims, our pocket money stretches to Hay deodorant and a toasted sandwich and the occasional fruit smoothie with cream: we want Marko and Bert, their haircuts and helmets, hairless faces, foreign goods on slender bodies and their little Vespas which whisk us off to the turquoise part of town.

Did you know that our folk in the Lora harbour district killed Boba's dad? That's the kind of story the south wind brought to us in the Valley of the First Menstruation from the Valley of the Geeks.

Boba is my neighbour, she's nine, her brother's six, their dad taught PE in the primary school, we all knew him, he was a strong man from the interior of the country, he was killed with fists, tortured and beaten. Even a strong man can succumb to injuries. Whenever I meet Boba's mum, a skinny woman called Anka, I turn dark red.

Why did I meet Anka today (twenty years ago), as I was hurrying to the Valley of the First Menstruation, this morning when the little streets I went down through the city to the sea were more exciting than underground streams. My streets with their high blue ceiling, clumps of flowers, fountains and birds, rivers of people in fluttery Italian shirts and light trousers ... I mumble good morning and blush horribly, good morning says Anka, looking me in the eye, with a slight smile, and quickly disappears, as long as no one calls her children Serbian Chetniks, we'll get by somehow, where can I go, all my people are from here, leave the kids alone, dear neighbours. Wow, Anka, why did I have to meet you today (twenty years ago), I remember when you weren't skinny, as though you'd escaped from a camp, your homeland is an everlasting camp, Anka, dear Ankica. Today (some twenty years later), in Lora the little girls do ballet, their small feet clatter gaily, the thud of a fist into flesh is muffled, the thud of a skull against a wall, they mostly dance vaudeville, the cry is muffled, applause muffles the screams of the one into whose throat acid is poured, encore covers over the one through whom electricity is run.

Our little slaughterhouse is now a cheerful stage.

People and town, flowers of the Mediterranean,

Life behind sunglasses,

I can't bear it, although I do, I walk faster. Marko and Bert are waiting, I'm on my way, take me away from this place, right now. I'm seventeen, it's 1995, but some streets are lovelier than a waterfall, and the sea is lovelier than a cathedral, fuck it. The war is nearly over, the war will never end, until we all die out. Even you and your Vespas.

'Hey, hat! You, hat, d'you hear? The hat can't hear, it's deaf. I'm calling you, girl.'

'Me?' I touch the brim of my little hat with my fingers. (I remember.)

'My mate Nightingale wants to meet you. That's him there, waving!'

He was leaning on a palm tree, as far as he could, smoking, one arm raised.

'Why?'

'You interest him.'

'If he's got something to say, let him come himself, there's no need for a mediator.'

'He says you should come, you hear. He's embarrassed, he's shy. What's your name, cute hat?'

'Clementine.'

'No shit!, Nightingale and Clementine, that's a sign. Freud would be beside himself.'

'Really?!! I'm waiting for someone and I can't just go off to meet people.'

'You're not waiting for Bert? He's not here, hon. Paying a visit. Joke. Come on, let's not 'juice you!'. Joke. D'you know who I am?'

I had noticed the Bosnian accent. I knew her from before, there had never been any bald girls in Split, the girls in Split mostly looked like clowns, pretty to some, but clowns all the same.

'Probably. Everyone knows you.'

She frightened me because she seemed fearless, naked as she was, bald, with a snake's body, unpredictable to me (always). She was (and remained) a head taller than me.

'Helanka, that's what people call me, damn their Mandril mothers' eyes. Pleased to meet you, I am Hela N-ka! Empress of Africa and Asia.'

That's how I met her, Helanka. And that's how, that morning, I met Nightingale.

LETTER FROM A WAR VETERAN

Sometimes at night I hear someone making love noisily, then when I open the windows, I light a cigarette and blow smoke into the darkness. (Otherwise I keep myself well shut up, I put on the air-conditioning and the TV, any programme that happens to be on so that I am not alone.)

Sometimes I amuse myself by trying to figure out which of you, my neighbours, is kissing.

For instance, I know a charmer from this street who used to hand out call-up notices but never saw the front line himself. I hope it isn't him. I don't hate him now, and I despise him ever less, I only remember him when I meet him in the street or a shop and say: 'hi.' But still, I hope he is not the one screwing. I hope that the fact that he handed out summonses to war in his Bermudas and flip-flops makes it hard for him to get it up. That would be poetic justice, but it never happens in reality, presumably because it is poetic, and not real justice. In reality, the surviving victims get cancer or diabetes, while the criminals get a new identity and Bermuda, the odd year behind bars, perhaps, some crack up, their nerves fray, they kill themselves, or their family and then themselves, but the thing with criminals is that they mostly don't have any nerves, not a single one, that's why their throat-cutting goes so well, neither their voice nor their hand trembles. I don't know what the people who hand out call-up notices get, what their bag is, but I'd like them not to get laid.

And the guy four floors down, a miserable wretch who exploited his uniform to break into the flat of someone in the army, and he's still living there – let girls not give him their pussies or men their cocks. Hey, women of Split, I yelled a few evenings ago from my window, please don't give the geezer from the fifth floor your pussies! No pussies for thieves! Then he called the police on me, he, the thief did, anonymously. Those people, the ones who stole in my name, make me cringe with shame, Mr Policeman, can't you see, they're disturbing my public peace and quiet!

I wanted to be the street's hero. But the war took me by surprise. There was nothing heroic about it. We were driving towards Dubrovnik, our unit was, and from the opposite direction, we were passed by a convertible with young people in it, including girls, we were driving along the old road, slowly, and I saw their faces, my contemporaries, maybe they were students, first or second year, like me, it was summer and Dubrovnik was at the end of the world.

Were they the street's heroes? They fucked their way through the war, you could see it like that. I didn't see it like that. But when I shat myself when I was hit in the legs by shrapnel from a shell – I was lying up to my neck in shit, I put my hands over my face and caught sight of my nails with blood congealing under them – then I thought about the girl in the convertible, I thought nice things about her, maybe that saved me, we were just lying on a beach and instead of blood and gunpowder, I had sand under my nails and on my finger tips a bit of sun screen from her back. Tropical Blend.

You have to get out of here, lad, said my commander when it was over. I have to get away from here. In the next war, if there is one while I'm still of military age, I'll be a deserter, I'll run away disguised as a woman, like one of my colleagues from Uni, then I'll drive a convertible, a dilapidated jeep or fine two-seater, next to a girl. Even if the enemy fires at the gates of my town, intending to burn and kill, even then I'll run away so as not to fire at my enemy.

I'm interested to know how I'll feel then when I drive with a girl in a convertible past soldiers driving on the other side of the road, knowing that they are going to war. Disgust with them or with myself? With them or myself? In some circumstances, that's the most terrible thing, you'll always be wrong, no matter what you do and that fateful bullet will follow you faithfully, you will feel it, whether it's fired or not, there's rust in your flesh as well.

Does the girl in the convertible ever remember that encounter on the road or did she quickly forget that by-passing of two worlds in a moment one afternoon? The girl was coming from paradise, I was going to hell, but at the same time, in the same place. When she glanced at me, in those few seconds, did she find me comical, disgusting, a stoned idiot, a potential butcher, appealing, perhaps a hero, did she feel uncomfortable or was I close and dear to her? Did I mean anything at all to her, a symbol, an emotion, to that delicate brunette with the wind tangling her hair and revealing her face and who a few days later, in the moments before death, became my life, the thought of her tossing me out of the blood and excrement into the light?

After some time I forgot everything to do with the war. For the most part, I shifted the dead and the devastation away and moved on, I decided – here's the university, a job, girls, a regular life, I handed over my weapons forever. When people ask I say I'm a worker or a sportsman, an engineer, a dad, a mountaineer, but not a soldier, you're a soldier in war and that's it, it's peacetime, you have to get out of the war through your head, because it's only through your head that you can get out, but like this, in the evening, when someone's making love, and I'm standing on my balcony looking at the sky in the dark, I remember that girl, a mirage on the road, almost unreal compared to fairly concrete death, but still invincible – such are illusions – and I think of myself, a second-year student, a soldier who didn't wish to die so that he might one day be able to rub her back with sun screen.

I'd like you, who are ardently making babies in the night, when you bring them into the world to tell them that there's nothing heroic about war, tell them that in passing, just in case, and repeat it several times.

At some stage, when school text books will contain the words *There is nothing heroic about war*, when newspapers publish headlines saying *There is nothing heroic about war*, when television announcers say *There is nothing heroic about war*, when generals come out in public with the military secret *There is nothing heroic about war*, when people proclaim from pulpits and minarets *There is nothing heroic about war*, when a war veteran whispers to his beloved as they lie naked as children *There is nothing heroic, or romantic, about war*, when directors produce a Hollywood film entitled *There is nothing heroic about war* (because a troop of fools in a real war come off better than a troop of wise men), then it really will be, after such a long time, important news.

And the soldiers will, willy-nilly, take off their boots and emerge from war, to carry on constructing a civilian life. Wherever they are.

An old warrior.

At that time I was living with my parents. I had been an only child for sixteen years, and then I acquired a brother (a doll, but not Pinocchio, he was a real boy!) and life turned head over heels (pirouette forward, pirouette backwards, *salto*, onto the head, onto the tum and again and again). I loved my brother instantly, but I couldn't bear the whole situation, the scrambling, yelling and constant chaos: dishes and laundry in dirty and clean heaps that kept growing. The child took over the flat (space, all available time), he banged on the door of my room, but in fact that didn't matter: I was forever plugged into my headset, so it all came to me too late or too early, in too small a flat.

But I loved, for instance, lying beside the sleeping baby and listening to him breathe. Rare moments, the remnants of a lost peace and relaxing domestic tedium: Dad asleep on the couch in the dining-room with his mouth open like a beached fish, Mum worn-out, her breasts half-bare, snoring softly beside the child.

My parents had no time for me, finally, and I began to feel some of the charms of freedom.

As soon as spring came (my seventeenth, fragrant and promising, but unhappy), I talked Dad into giving me the key of Grandpa's boat. Then (twenty years ago, yes, so much time has passed) the boat was called a dinghy and it had been on dry land since Grandpa's death. 'But I've got nowhere to study', I told my father, 'can't you see it's impossible in the flat, I'll go crazy, it'd drive anyone crazy.' And he put the boat back in the sea, into life, maybe more for his own sake, because he always hoped that we'd sail away some time, he wanted to see the Kornati islands again… but it didn't happen.

This gave him hope: he took Grandpa's rusty tins and filthy rags out, we cleaned the inside, there was always a stink of sea-sickness: a mixture of oil and stagnant salt water and the rotting sun of past summers, but the main thing was that it was dry ("as a ducat," as Grandpa used to say), the table was big enough, you could study, the WC functioned, there was an electric ring for tea/coffee, we put clean bedding on the old foam mattress in the cabin, even untangled the long line (Dad), while he swore profusely and gaily (all the while), cleaned the seaweed and congealed pieces of squid off the hooks and put it away in the store in the stern. But he never sailed away, poor Dad.

At first I really did study on the boat, yes, yes. And read Grandma's romances, *My Destinies* and *My Secrets*, the only reading matter along with a channel guide and two thin kiosk cookbooks with which she had filled the boat's library (a refuge from Grandpa's reticence in the long, tedious hours of sailing and amateur fishing, a bit of dynamism and passion for Grandma after endless jerking with a sharp transparent line as they hunted for squid); I also wrote a few poems, with rhymes, went out, roamed, met up with friends (the days were sometimes enchanting, because there were no nights), but I did study, I was a good child (that last year) and I paid for my precious freedom with good marks; I didn't let anyone in under the prow, not even Bert.

Bert had long straight black hair at that time, parted in the centre, and a long head, he spoke slowly and morosely, as though he couldn't be bothered about anything, but with a smile, a smile that flickered in the corner of his eye, at the edge of his mouth; he was a popular kid, my Bert, critical and dissatisfied with people, the world and the rest of the universe. That was so that the universe should not show itself to be dissatisfied with him (self-defence, attack is the best defence). It's true that I often felt bored in his company, but that boredom was not disagreeable. In those days I was chosen, for he was choosy, and more in love with that fact than with his fingers and voice (fingers with long nails and a pleasant voice and genuinely lovely, warm eyes), but as though it matters where it comes from, love is always powerful and endless as long as it lasts.

We kissed on the sea rocks and explored each other's underpants, blind with petting, but when things heated up, I was ashamed to invite him onto the boat. He, on the other hand, was not ashamed to take me to a field shed on a chicken farm belonging to some relative of his. I lost my virginity on a mattress thrown over sacks of hybrid maize, while hens clucked under lamps next door.

'Oh,' said Bert, as though he was a bit surprised by my obstacle. Let's get this over, I thought, then let a big love begin.

Through an opening in the door I caught sight of a star above a reed bed gently ruffled by a breeze, dew sparkled in the darkness, and a bird could be heard calling somewhere high on the hill. There was a soft warmth and floury smell in the hut, his hair (finally dishevelled) on my face, a radio played good songs in the night, our naked bodies, so young and full of torment, unliberated pleasure. We had all that.

It wasn't good, it was too like a battle for something delectable and painful, but unfathomable to us, but I had heard that the first time was never any good for anyone.

He took me home on his Vespa (again the moon over the reed bed swaying in the breeze, dew in the darkness, the song of a night bird, his hair on my cheek, in vain), we hardly said goodbye, he didn't call me again, or I him, something had shamed us like an illness, a month later I met him with a tall girl, as long as him, they were holding hands – he had never wanted to hold my hand, and that rankled. 'What the f…,!' I said, I didn't even swear at that time, and I wished him dead (my crushed and bloody vain child's heart was floundering in the mud, snarling and shrieking by turn).

There, that's all I knew about love at the time I met Nightingale. Grandma's romances and one not exactly successful sex act, along with several inconsequential tourist droolings on benches and beaches, and that's it.

I didn't go down to the Valley of the First Menstruation any more. Life didn't offer me anything much, but it promised all sorts of brilliant bullshit, while the future didn't yet have a limit, in fact the future didn't even exist. Young people live as though they are immortal, that's why youth is so good even when it's quite bad.

A few years later (the burn had cooled) I met Robert the lawyer (the former Bert) in Zagreb, he had cut his hair, and on that smooth face a fine short, thick beard had grown (I remember, it felt odd to the touch), he was well-dressed and he smelled good (he always had as far as I recall). It was inevitable: we liberated that childish shamefaced pleasure of its torments. Impeccable as a young cat, Bert became my second husband.

The first was Gale. The not remotely impeccable Nightingale.

Maybe love can't be avoided, and maybe that youthful marriage wouldn't have happened, my dear, and it could be that I wouldn't have got entangled with Gale had Dad not been falling apart at that time (roughly twenty years ago).

His condition, following several flashes in his brain (he described them as flashes) was shockingly like a short circuit. At times he would temporarily lose his sight, in mid-step, and fall onto his knees. To start with he was terrified among shadows and outlines, but later he got used to it, and he used to read newspaper headlines with a big magnifying glass (for butterflies or bugs or philately, I don't know, I don't know its function) held up to his eye. Later his sight would come back for a while, but whole people would vanish from his memory: for instance some important family event was preserved, but Ma would have dropped out of it, or there were occasions when I, his daughter, would move for a few days into his past, moving right out of the present (on those days he would leave me without dinner, having eaten my portion as well as his own), and one Sunday my little brother became his own younger brother, although he didn't himself have any brothers, or sisters. They were strange situations, but worse were the times he became a seagull with red cheeks standing on one leg, in an attempt at flying, a fat seagull that was laughing. Mum would turn her back towards the kitchen and I could see her shoulders shaking, with tears and laughter, especially when the hundred-kilo bird peed itself. That comic dimension in a personal tragedy does not mitigate it – as in some story – everything becomes even more tragic, life moves into the grotesque. But life is life, and this is a story about life.

The world with its street where in rainy weather water drips loudly from the gutters, with its town in which dogs crap and people spit relentlessly, with its country sunk up to its neck in a filthy little war – all of that, which is why I mention it, used to really bother Dad – it all vanished from his focus. A little shred of reality fluttered on the margins of his new consciousness, but didn't fundamentally disturb his view of a surreal tropical postcard, which he presented to us increasingly often.

When the paramedics sometimes came for him, he used to tell them, very coherently, the same story: it was a story about four girls, who had waited for him one distant unripe summer, or perhaps spring or autumn, because in places beside warm seas, as the years pass, it's always just one season in the memory, the past becomes eternal summer (perhaps in Aspen the past is eternal winter, what do you think?), even in Dad's case where all his thoughts were shrouded in white emptiness. Out of that otherworldly emptiness the last to step were the four girls (Mirjana, Sabina, Alenka and Apotekarica) in summer sandals and he, tender and multiplied fourfold, hugged them one after the other with his boyishly large bare arms of a future sailor and led them, protected like this, to the end of the promenade into an August evening. So, in their embrace or arm in arm, he strolled out of his present, and later out of his consciousness altogether, and then out of life itself.

Somewhere, in all probability, and long ago, Mirjana, Sabina, Alenka and Apotekarica had more or less agreeable lives in the fold of those close to them, and, interestingly enough, they weren't so much as grazed by Dad's unexpected departure into emptiness with them in his thoughts, while in our flat, high on the ninth floor in Šimunović Street, Ma was left utterly alone. As well as being strange, it was unjust. The fact that two children sat there with her made her, if it was possible, still more alone. The endless white universe that had poured into Dad's head with a crash, then silently overflowed into Ma's huge heart and leaked all through the room where we three orphans sat staring at one another.

And then I too, villainously, on tiptoe, stole out of that world into the more appealing one that awaited me down in the harbour. I dreamed up ways of earning small change for the things that were important to me: I began writing stories modelled on Grandma's romances. That year I wrote six, the following year thirteen. Although I was uninformed about love, I was deft with words, I was able to make a lot out of a little. *My Secret* and *My Destiny* valued my sense of drama. They valued it as did some big publishers. Cash flowed. Broom and jasmine spread their scent, crazily, everything was being renewed, that spring and summer I grew to my full extent and as though anxieties, illness, wars and deaths didn't touch me, everything drove me onward, all the sirens strove to summon me (those from the sea and those in cars and those announcing the end of air raids) and I said yes, yes, oh yes ... oh, yes.

LETTER FROM A LITTLE GIRL
WHO DOES NOT WANT TO FALL IN LOVE

I knew what was going on, I'd never heard noises like that before, but I knew that was it. I once saw two dogs in our street, I sat down on a wall and pretended I was playing *Mmm Fingers* on a smart phone, but in fact I had sat there because I was mesmerised by the mating dogs, although I was ashamed and it looked genuinely disgusting, like what I saw last summer at the lighthouse above the nudist beach. Although our beach, immediately below the lighthouse, had only topless women, one morning I had gone to that other beach nearby, concealed by rocks, and saw completely naked people, not only without anything on their top half, but without anything on their bottom half either. I promised myself that I would never go there again, but the next day, as soon as my parents were busy with something else, I set off for a walk and somehow my feet took me in that direction of their own accord. The following evening I promised myself again that I would go just the next day and then never again, that would be the last time. The whole morning I waited for my parents to start making lunch, to forget about me for a bit and I got bored watching a goby in the shallows that had fallen in love with my big toe. As soon as they forgot about me, I set off barefoot along a little path that was full of burrs and thorns, because I didn't want to go into my room for my flip-flops in case my mother asked me something, or my father, even worse. The earth burned the soles of my feet, it was full of ants, and the pebbles bruised me and I didn't manage to get far or see much. I went home cross and very tired from the sun.

'Where you been' asked my cousin – he's a year older than me – 'in this noonday sun?'

'Picking blackberries, on the hill,' I came up with.

'Picking blackberries at midday!' he retorted. 'Did you see the starkers people?' 'No. Yes. Yes, I saw them. So what?'

'Come here,' he said, pointing to a pine tree from which you could watch the nudists without them seeing you.

In the afternoon we took some other children with us. And the two next days as well. But by the third day I wasn't interested any more, because the other children laughed, and the boys talked rubbish like, they're nude so they can fuck. It was no longer terrible or interesting as it had been when I was alone and I gave up watching the starkers people. Fortunately, because the next day they sent the nudist beach warden to the other children's parents and their parents whacked them. And so it passed, and only some images stayed in my mind, and I thought about them after swimming when I'd lie on my belly, on my towel, with my forehead and palms on the hot concrete. Later I'd put my feet in the water and wait for the crazy goby. Dad watched a sun-tanned woman with big tits coming out of the sea and said to Ma, 'Isn't she a looker?' 'She's lovely,' said Ma, quietly in amazement. 'You're both cracked,' I said and strode off to my room. If that had something to do with love, I didn't want ever to fall in love. And let those crazy people outside shut up forever. I'm not afraid of you.

But, hey, he's stolen this story from me. It's my story that I told him, about the summer at the lighthouse above the nudist beach. He remembered it. But in fact I wouldn't have been able to write it like that, although Gale used to say that I had more talent than he did, only I wasted it on stupidities. But he ate the biscuits we bought with those stupidities. (I feel like a child eating his pet slaughtered lamb, my Gale used to say.) And he remembers everything, as I do. Or rather, as I did, before. As though that mattered now, dear, madness. Madness is nice.

I've come to terms with it, I'm just someone who writes romances, television lemonade that one critic renamed orangeade because of my name. I thought that was witty. There was never any reason to care about criticism from those worse and stupider than me, so I wrote soaps, not novels. I had and still have enough bourgeois comfort, sometimes even glamour, and that's what I achieved, and that means something today. And I settled all my bills myself. Lots and lots of biscuits.

So, let me get back to the road. When I finally came off the main road onto a minor one and forty minutes later reached the village of Tulumbe (I've been here for the last ten days) – once an Orthodox village in Bosnia, now a green wasteland – I was met by those children. I had been expecting possibly a granddad, or a dog, or a sheep, or a wild animal. I was never much good with children (my brother, who fell into the sea several times in my care, can confirm that, sweetheart). You never know what they're going to do next, children, it's better to leave them to someone with more concentration.

However, it's a fact, I realise this: everyone has his child. For some their child is a dog, for someone else a cat, or a partner, some people are their own children, for some it's their job, for some it's their convertible, and for some a daughter or son. Like all parents without children, I sometimes wonder what he or she would have looked like? (A daughter who resembles Gale, for instance.) I shall never treat my non-existent daughter to my absence, irritation, quarrels, separation, bad food, bad education, maybe even a war or a camp, statistically that's very likely, it gets us every other generation, she won't be blown up on a school trip by a terrorist, she won't kill herself on the underground, she won't be endlessly bored, she won't be abused by school mates or some jerk of a boss, she won't be raped or beaten up, she won't feel lonely, depressed, a failure, no one will break her heart, she won't live an average life, she won't be crushed by some mediocrity whom she'd probably end up marrying, she won't die of a disease or in some banal accident, and some of that would have happened, maybe all of it. I couldn't explain that to Bert. It's not possible to be a good parent if you want to be something else as well. And I wanted that something else. People produce children, then they're brought up by unknown women in rooms stuffed with kids, rooms which stink a bit of children's urine. I suppose that in a few decades, at the latest in a hundred years' time, there won't be any families but family organisations like mini tribal communities, where everyone will take care of the children, as used to be the case with whole villages (incestuous villages, admittedly). The children will be cared for by concerned parents, not necessarily biological, but those who're gifted and trained for this essential, life-long job. Talented professional fathers, well-paid professional mothers, people of great emotional intelligence, mild and firm, warm and sympathetic, and for several decades there'd be no maniacs, or paedophiles, or soldiers. I've seen enough young actresses who thought it was sweet; they bought up-market prams and disappeared from the stage for a while, the first was followed by a second, they came back ten kilos heavier, demented by the domestic regime, their husband, their children, some disappeared forever, the cleverer ones divorced, had their tits and tums operated on and came back. But in vain, youth passes in the blink of an eye. Or the crack of a whip. My darling non-existent daughter, with clear eyes, with a slightly protruding right ear that sticks out through your hair, with a freckled nose and wonderful smile, you won't watch me get married and divorced, go downhill, get fat, get old, neglect my hygiene, you won't run away from me, you won't live with me, I won't watch you get married and divorced, go downhill, get fat, get old, neglect yourself as well, you won't forget me and you won't break my heart, I won't say I don't love you (or I love you, either, for that matter). Everyone knows this, but then again everyone thinks: being born is after all better than not being born. And you would have liked me to give birth to you, wouldn't you?

There was no sign announcing Tulumbe, but I recognised the village by the Red School beside the road, from Helanka's account. I sometimes forget the name of foods or individual letters, but not some unearthly images I've never even seen. A red building with no windows, a large cut-out, regular single-storey block, a cube of blood on soft green felt, merging with the low sky above the valley. Behind the school I came across an arrow made out of wood with *Tulumbe* written on it, I left the tarmac road and followed the tracks of a large vehicle across a meadow, towards a house in the valley at the bottom of a hill. The morning was sunny and fresh, and I drove myself straight into the low blue sky.

Those two already-grown children, with light, almost white hair, the same height and build – blue-eyed, skinny grasshoppers – met me in the meadow. They surfaced from somewhere in the wheat and ran like Indians after my car. Billy Goat and Arrow, Helanka's children (it turned out). At first I thought they were a boy and a girl, but they were actually twin girls. Billy Goat put me right in a matter-of-fact way, smiling, by way of proof, she had defiant thirteen year-old tits under her striped t-shirt. 'I'm a tomboy,' she explained solemnly, her hands on her hips (I had got out of the car and they were examining it inquisitively). Billy Goat had big scabs on her elbows (from falling off the mule, she said), and her hair was cut very short. Arrow was different. A gentler copy of her sister (her gentleness was in her movements, her gestures), a quiet girl with an elusive expression under long eyelashes, with silken hair over her shoulders and a small fireman's axe in her hand – she followed us quietly to the house.

In front of a gate made of unhewn branches stood a fine wooden sign: *Tulumbe Eco Estate*. ('The two of us made it,' said the boy-twin. Arrow added that Gramps had *helped*. 'And Jusuf.') Meadows and forests stretched for miles around, with deer, foxes and bears roaming through them, like several thousand years ago when there weren't any people here, just as there aren't now, actually, since the end of the war.

'Helanka's not at home and we aren't sure when she'll be back,' said Billy Goat. Apparently, Helanka goes from time to time to the nearest small town or even to some larger town for deliveries (she sells cheese, wool, honey, mushrooms, raspberry juice and magical juniper brandy) and for supplies and comes back after a day or two, sometimes three, sometimes even five, with industrial quantities of food, necessities and memory sticks for the Internet ('Have you got a stick?' was the only thing Arrow asked me that first day, and at that moment I didn't know what she meant). Helanka is now like the mother of two Rapunzels with short hair, she has confined them, her daughters, to a remote vanished village (a non-existent village) over the holidays, while she saunters through the valleys and mountains, filling her pouch to bursting point.

Sometimes people come to them, 'Mum calls them clients, for food, for herbs for teas, for Mum's potions that can cure everything.' Behind the house is Helanka's medicinal garden (the girls have written that on a rough-cut wooden board, the little darlings), with quantities of mountain plants, but also basil, rosemary, sage, lavender, oregano, tall stems of marijuana, foreign Mediterranean plants that don't otherwise grow in this greasy black soil (the crazy mother brought special earth for them, a whole truck full). Little blue butterflies have covered the garden and the meadow that is its natural continuation. The aromas compete, cold oils merge with hot ones, juices mix and couple. On a little path is the signpost to the house: brown pebbles, grassy horse droppings.

On a rise, under a few young pines, are a tall shed, a narrow pen, a wooden barn, an orchard full of over-ripe blue plums with swarms of insects teeming round them and small rotting apples, a wooden trough with a little murky water in it along with hay dropped from cows and horses' mouths, a freshly whitewashed well for rain-water, a little hut made of logs and quicklime, on its own and small, but new, repaired, with windows opening wide towards the black top of the mountain, perfectly alive in the middle of nothing. Billy Goat scuttled behind the house and started the generator, while Arrow (only then did she put down her small axe) warmed a little milk (they milked the cow themselves) and water for tea (or it was the other way round, Arrow started the generator, while Billy Goat …).

Whatever. I settled down on the wide wooden bench in the kitchen, called 'a settee' they told me (as though I didn't know). I unpacked my things, very strange in those surroundings.

'What's this?' they asked me. They had never seen a dictaphone. 'What's it for?'

'It records voices, and the battery lasts far longer than an iPhone's. Here, I'll show you. May I record you?'

'Yes!'

'Yes.'

'What shall I ask you? Does anyone keep an eye on you when Mum's away?'

'Gramps! He's up on the hill.'

'Gramps and Granma. And Jusuf.'

'They live on the hill, they get a signal, because of the weather station, we go up there every day, and they let us use the computer too. They make food for us, bring us home after supper and lock us in until morning. When Mum's not here. They aren't our real grand-parents, but they always look after us. Gramps and Granma, get it?'

'And Jusuf, Billy.'

'And Jusuf, they look after him, he's simple. Even though he's old. And Granma's a bit daft as well.'

'About forty.'

'Why, that's really old, dear. Who helped you with the house?'

'Jusuf.'

'No he didn't, Gramps did more, so did we. And Dad came. Have you fallen in love with Jusuf, you idiot?'

'No, you idiot. He sisted.'

'Assisted.'

'Sisted! Sisted!'

'Just let mother come home as soon as possible, we have no time when she's away. We have to make a new clip. We're bloggers, YouTubers. We have to post stuff regularly, or people will stop following us.'

'Aha, okay, my dear. What are you called on YouTube?'

'You can find us. We're called Meri and Tea.'

'Not Billy Goat and Arrow?'

'Nooo, no. Although I like Billy Goat. It's not sweet or contrived. And I like hers – Arrow – too. Because it's powerful and precise, like her.'

'So what do you do on YouTube, dear?'

'Arrow plays chess with the computer and always wins. I film her. She plays with grand masters, only virtually. That's how we began. To prove what morons they are in the club who won't let her play against men. We keep challenging new opponents, but they mostly don't answer. We've just challenged the Pope.'

'The Pope? Really?'

'Yes. We filmed a challenge to the Pope in order to point out the position of women in the church. And there's a basis. Pope Francis might react. What do you think?'

'It'd attract viewers, Billy.'

'Indeed. And I also have lots of viewers because I'm good at making things, paper boats, planes, flowers, frogs, and also hairstyles, so I teach people to make hairstyles. It's not so important, but it's fun.'

'That's important too, Billy. What would people look like without hairstyles?'

'Like Mum? Arrow is my model most of the time.'

'Do you go to school?'

'Yes. But we sometimes miss the first week back. I think that'll happen this year as well.'

'I agree.'

'What about in winter?'

'In winter we live in Split, at Dad's, when it's school. Mum sometimes lives at Dad's, with us, it depends.'

'Danny-Boy is your Dad? So they told me right.'

'Yep.'

'Sometimes Mum stays here by herself in Tulumbe over the winter if there's a lot of snow or if she's travelling. Does that record onto a cassette? This Dictaphone?'

'Do you want to hear?'

'Yes.'

'You bet. Ace.'

'Mega Ace. I've never seen one. It's a bit old-fashioned.'

'Where d'you get it?'

'In Zagreb, a long time ago. When I was living there.'

'Then they must have them in Split. Are you going to record something else?'

'Yes, my dear. I'm going to record everything on this journey of mine. So I can remember this when I've forgotten everything else.'

'Ace. Mega.'

Helanka was lying on the couch in our flat in Šimunović Street between two flowery sheets of my mother's, which I brought as my dowry. That was before I moved to Zagreb, not long after Nightingale and I had suddenly fallen in love, erupted and got married. Gale had slipped out of bed in the middle of the night. Where had he gone? On some short trip. An exhibition of post-Yugoslav cartoons in Graz. A panel discussion of the political and the erotic in contemporary poetry in Ljubljana. Art and War – a lecture in Berlin. It could have been something like that. That night I had fallen asleep on top of him and he woke me when he moved my head onto the pillow. I was aware of the good smell of coffee and tobacco, and heard the sounds of a quiet conversation between him and Helanka in the kitchen. When my bladder obliged me to wake up properly, Gale had already flown out of the door. On my way back to the bedroom from the toilet I glimpse the glow of a cigarette from the couch. Helanka is smoking with her eyes closed. I sit down on the edge of the three-seater. You're not asleep? Lie down beside me. I lie down and feel that she is naked. Why are you naked? I always sleep naked. You should try it. I take her half-smoked cigarette from her and put it out, then I kiss her, between her lips, on her teeth. I kiss her, she doesn't stir.

'May I look at you, I ask?'

'No,' she says. 'You may not.'

'But I've already seen you on the boat,' I say in surprise (this was twenty years ago), but in fact I'm pretending to be surprised. Other people too are naked when they get undressed, but not as completely naked as Helanka.

'Go or come,' she says, opening her eyes. 'Come. Or go.'

I go to my room, and later hear something heavy hit my door. In the morning I find a broken ashtray.

'Did you throw it at my door? Or had you run out of cigarettes?' I ask her in the morning. She's making coffee with her back to me.

'Forgive me for last night, I don't know what came over me,' I say with a laugh.

'There's nothing to forgive, either way, we were larking about,' she says, still not turning round, she doesn't want to look at me.

That same day, later on, I read in some magazine the confession of a well-known French woman writer, to whom it happened, said the article, that when she was madly in love she ran out into the street in an intoxicated state and, full of love, fell in love with several other people she happened to meet. Like an infection. Helanka liked her books and I thought of showing her the article, but I thought it might not be clever. I showed it to Gale. He said, as though sensing what was troubling me: 'why that's normal, we fall in love with all our friends at first, luckily it doesn't last long, or there'd be chaos.' I didn't tell him about the episode with Helanka, and nor did she, as far as I know. We saw each other virtually every day, but I don't think she ever stayed the night again. We would sit on the balcony, play cards and look at the city and the sea, the windows of skyscrapers and roofs of buildings. On a deserted balcony a seagull was looking after and feeding several young grey gulls. Washing was drying, aerials stood straight up between the sea and the sky, the smell of braised onions reached us, domestic quarrels, sometimes the sound of a ship's siren. Sometimes I would see Anka, she would lean on her window, looking upwards. (Usually, people look down, from a window or a balcony.)

Helanka said, 'I'd kill myself if I was her, but she won't, she's got children.' 'Don't talk crap,' said Gale.

'Don't you talk crap,' said Helanka.

'Don't talk crap, both of you,' I said twenty years ago.

I waved briefly to Anka when I noticed she was looking our way. I saw her a few more times at her window, she always looked towards us for a long time, but she never waved back. I remember those days as though through polished glass. Everything moved slowly and routinely in the flat in Šimunović Street, not much faster or much more thickly than particles of dust in the afternoon sun. As though that morning nothing had happened, because, apparently nothing had.

LETTER FROM THE GHOST
OF DINKO ŠIMUNOVIĆ

At first I thought they were seagulls, sea birds calling, but what I was hearing was a song of amorous sighs. Although I was caught off guard, as I walked down the street which for some unknown reason bears my name – when I lived in this town there was no street here – just brambles, fennel, a field – I stopped, listened and youthful vigour and cheerfulness poured into my heart. I almost skipped with such exuberance.

In my lifetime, I despised modern culture and urban civilisation. I wanted tradition to be preserved, with the charm of poetry, legend and dreaming. Oh, how far away that all is now, as though it had never existed. How wrong I was ... But should I regret it now that I'm dead?

In my youth, when I began to seethe with an abundance of emotion and energy, I nourished my hunger for depth of feeling and beauty of thought on the wonderful pages of Pushkin, Gogol, Turgenev, Dostoevsky, Tolstoy, Goncharov, Saltykov-Shchedrin, Potapenko, and that transported me but also (for a long time) drove me away from the thought of writing something myself. All I read seemed so inaccessible.

But the town, the town brought me closer to accessible things. The town brought the village close to me the way a mirror is brought up to a face and I saw clearly what I had been blindly fumbling towards from childhood: that where the heart is not free there cannot be love.

These tall buildings and skyscrapers were inhabited by the children, grandchildren and great-grandchildren of my gentle characters from the harsh karst landscape. In these towns, which are now their homeland, they have no need to be unhappy any more. They need not be, if they do not wish to be. Their hearts can beat more freely, if that is what they want.

How much joy is love in itself! A desire for life rather than ambition, rather than a desire for power. It is the only utopia left to us. Around it stretches a black sea of indifference in which millions have drowned. For this reason, the chirping and cheeping in the darkness does not represent for me mere bodily union, although, I admit, perhaps that is what it is, for me it is a roar of life in this dark, silent box of the night from which there is no way out other than through this tiny rip of sound. And, since there is such a tear, scratched out, the little flames of other light will penetrate through it into this silent world: music and footsteps, whispers and conversation through a kiss. Murmuring: the pulse of the town. I see now, the street is the site of new poetry, legend and dreaming, and streets are the town.

What could I write about now, at a time of greater freedom, at least for some? I see that our writers are still weighed down by shortages and moral humiliations, and it is hard for such people to write, hardest of all novellas which must be imbued with fresh poetry, beauty, love and youthful smiles. That smile can be a bit mocking or impish, sometimes bitter or mixed with tears, but it should always come from a tender soul. It is good to write from an outpouring of love, rather than of vengeance and hatred even about the last ugly things. I have read new books and in them I have found a great deal of contemporary people's justified fury. I postulate that if love disappears as a literary obsession, all we will be left with, as topics, will be injustice and death. If books are a reflection of the world, is it really the case that in the entire world only injustice has remained important and serious? (Because death, we will admit to ourselves, at least in secret, is not taken seriously, apart from our own losses.)

Here the letter comes to a sudden end.

Which means, our good Dinko, that you wrote a few excellent stories and deserve a street, my dear, just such an epic-lyric one (although no one knows why it is you it is named after), but the town is *passé*. The town is on the way out. The community for which it came into being is too. The world is moving to the suburbs, to live its life there, alone, isolated, in peace and on social networks. The poor move to industrial suburbs, the rich to green elite ones or to new villages, villages inhabited by townsfolk, with education and deeper pockets. I always remember those allotments with a little hut for tools and a few square metres of earth on the way out of Berlin, which I saw some years ago. Townsfolk have a need to scrabble in the soil.

Before the townsfolk move out, or perhaps at the same time, the towns will be taken over by tourist apartments, banks, business and shopping centres, expensive shops and pizzerias. Towns will become museums, many already are. Split too will become a museum, sweetheart. And a destination, in the summer for ordinary tourists, and in the winter for the inhabitants from both the poor and the wealthy suburbs. It will survive as a stage set, for celebrating feast days, festivals, fairs and pre-election rallies. People will come to town to be in touch with each other several times a year. I don't believe that Nightingale can't see this. (Or had he simply wanted to give a convincing voice to a dead writer? And maybe he was even mocking him.) For Gale, his district and street are his chosen homeland, so his letters are probably a kind of homage to such a town, before he abandoned it, while the town still existed in its full strength – although its future could already be seen, I would say.

What will become of my towns? In addition to Split, I had many towns in which I lived for shorter or longer spells, in some for two or three days, in some for years. And Zagreb, especially Zagreb.

It's already early autumn there, different from the one here: witches trudge through the leaves on Strossmayer Square, they hide under benches and slip their small hands into anyone's moist underpants, and then they turn into mist and steam and follow couples who, after some amorous petting, scuttle smiling into a smoky, warm corner for soup or tea and as they imbibe it, the witches settle on their lips. Unlike my acquaintances who find it annoying, because they care, I owe nothing to Zagreb other than comfort. Sometimes in my thoughts it rolls along in front of my feet, sometimes it raps me on the head. Zagreb is my chestnut. (It's autumn there.) Although I spent important years there, I was always by my own choice a tourist in Zagreb. Savouring it in passing. Thanks to my inclination to enjoyment, to success in things that were important to me at that time, I avoided the incarceration of ordinary love, habit and need, which is so easily transformed into frustration.

My Zagreb years, I should not gloss over them, were years of tranquillity and certain privileges, post-war years, a time when it still appeared that the worst had passed (the worst never passes, it seems, it is just pacified). That late autumn when I first arrived intoxicated me. In the early autumn in Zagreb, people are fresher at the beginning, full of plans, how different that is from the Dalmatian autumn that is the end of everything. It isn't surprising that people from the sea fall in love with Zagreb, it's so logical and natural, when life ceases in our homeland we move to another homeland, like birds.

In the opposite direction from birds, but with a similar logic. And then comes the aroma of a long winter, cold that steams the breath: pink cheeks, the heat of inside spaces. But I was warmed by love, my young marriage that had remained down at the sea and to which I could return whenever I wanted and I did that constantly, hungrily. With equal gaiety with which at the end of the weekend I returned to Zagreb and my job.

At the beginning of those years, my relationship with Gale was in the distance, full of love and resentment, nocturnal journeys by bus along the old coast road, morning arrivals, afternoons squashed under a sheet in the boat's cabin, in winter in a room with a view of the town and the sea, and returning that same evening in which the night was always shorter, and the coast road longer, than when I was arriving, then after a break, a carefree marriage to Bert, without great passion, comradely, with good comradely sex, with a nice shared flat in an elite district and corresponding credit, with no children, with enough money, with two extramarital affairs on my part (I don't have much to remember of that now, so it's better in future not to remember).

First there was that phone call: 'Would you write a screenplay? We found you through *My Secrets* or *Destinies*, the editor didn't want to give us your contacts, but you would be most welcome on our team.'

'But I've never written a screenplay.'

'That's OK, it's quickly learned, we have experienced people here, think about it, it would be useful for us to have someone who knows the Dalmatian dialect.'

'Do you mean the Split dialect?'

'But let us know on Friday.'

'But Friday's tomorrow.'

'Yes, that's right, tomorrow, we need to know as soon as possible, tomorrow, we have to record the first twenty episodes by the end of April.'

'But it's April now.'

'Yes that's right, it's April, it's a punishing schedule, best not to be surprised.'

'But I live in Split, well, yes, I could come to Zagreb for a meeting, I could, just give me a little time to consider.'

The next day I accepted, of course. For a kid with no father, who had just left school, with a teacher mother and a little brother, with an unemployed husband, a poet and military deserter, this was, let's face it, a ticket to Hawaii or, maybe, to Hollywood.

When their main co-screenwriter fell ill (in fact she ran away), I immediately leapt into her place (I was never pushy, I had the requisite skills, so there was no need to push). I became, let's say, a little harder to replace than the others. Thanks to my enviable production of romances, I typed well, as a former eager beaver I had a solid acquaintance with the basic concepts of general culture, I had always had a fertile imagination, I didn't have a regular job, nor money for studying or acquiring a qualification. But even later: I was married for a second time to a young future lawyer, he was never at home (especially when he got a job in a bank), I didn't want children, I needed a fiercer and briefer love (I didn't know that then, of course, it was a belated realisation), and writing gave me a feeling of being in love, I could write for hours the way people in love can have sex for hours, the way those people in Gale's letters screw all night long. That's how I wrote, like running water, there was no time for abandoning the game, other than for sleep, maybe food, until the weekend. In a word, I was as though made for this work – too good. At first all I needed was a coffee or tea and a cigarette, later it was – later. Never overdone, I mean the stimulants, because I was afraid of losing control.

The words poured out of me, I knew at once, the most important thing was to abandon yourself to it. And later you relax, think up the beginning, let others elaborate, serve their apprenticeships. At that time I also met the magic Kalemengo, the daddy of showbiz. I started using Dictaphones (later sometimes also smartphones), I had hundreds of cassettes, I talked, recorded, anywhere, as I walked, driving, in bed, in front of the television, and they (some kids, students) typed it all up, brought it to me to check. I worked constantly, tirelessly, my fingers swelled with writing. I was just twenty-six when I finally gave up my half-dream of university (I had attended, barely, just two semesters of comparative literature and philosophy), because reality looked good enough and required the whole of me, my darling. Money excited me, with money in my pocket I could realise dreams, other dreams, ones I had not even dreamed of.

My little star shone in newsagents' displays.

I wrote, first, the script for *Miljenko and Dobrila*, based on the legend of the unhappy lovers from Kaštel Lukšić, a little place near Split. We sold that to foreigners, in seventeen countries, which was a national record as far as TV series go, my dear. Although no one said so then (but they stress it today), my soap was in large part responsible for the restoration of the local hotel, tourists began stopping to visit the castles where the lovers lived, and the beautiful little (Renaissance?) church where they are buried together, with the words *Peace to the lovers* engraved on the stone. There is no reliable proof of the existence of Romeo and Juliet, while the undoubtedly real Miljenko and Dobrila waited for centuries to be discovered and here we are, my dear. Some of the biggest tourist shrines are based on fantasy, from Verona to Medjugorje or Disneyland. For their diversion, I offered even a little more excitement: I reimagined something that was real, I steeped an infinitely lovely and tragic story in romance (less tragic than in reality), which could be chewed over at length.

Gale, an orthodox artist, sent me a text message at that time: *Don't you feel uncomfortable, love? Why poor Miljenko and Dobrila? For God's sake!*

I tried not to respond. But I couldn't hold out, and justified myself. *(Why should I justify myself to you of all people? What do you do – you write a blog! And draw graffiti.)*

Then in two or three years, *Adel and Mara*, about the forbidden love between a young Turk and a girl from Split. A co-production with the Turks and Italians. 'A hit! We have a hit, Piccola!' My producer, Kalemengo, said that, walking up and down through the studio, like a coach. At a match. A European hit, he said, a world hit. But not even Kalemengo could have imagined what the series would become. I had uncovered a trick, by accident: an historical model with a love story (and the history could also come from some distant future): a forbidden love, good costumes, that was what people had adored since time began. Through the whole history of film and literature, that's largely all that people loved (you don't have to be particularly wise, I was never wise, I just followed my instinct). 'The artful think artfully, artists make artistry.' Kalemengo quoted the great Croatian writer Krleža. While poor Krleža turned a bit in his grave.

The ultimate result of it all was – and no one expected this, how could they – the founding of several new departments of the Croatian language in the wide world, in places where they did not use subtitles, for instance Japan! Just at the time when those departments were beginning to close, among other things because they had acquired a bad reputation, as I was told by a journalist who was doing a radio interview with me (and for a serious newspaper, for its cultural column, my dear). Our philologists exerted themselves fanatically on behalf of linguistic purity so it was easier for people who wanted to learn Croatian to learn Serbian rather than neo-Croatian, that's what the journalist told me, a greying and somewhat exhausted latent revolutionary. In the war years people were afraid of speaking their own language, some idiot would always pop up to correct you. Our tongue became so wooden that it could not be salvaged even by five generations of writers, added my journalist to his theme after we had lain tired and sweating (but certain about everything that a tongue could do) in bed, and he lit a cigarette for himself, then for me – a writer in our own and related idioms. And that journalist of mine was right, we were all lost in translation, only Helanka still spoke doggedly the way she always had in her Serbian/Croatian/Bosnian dialect, but she was in any case written off as a refugee.

My work protected me also from such grammatical poverty. We had a market (this world is prodigious, even commerce is virtual, there is nothing more real than a simulacrum), and the market did not tolerate the frontiers of small nations. Soaps were a place of natural and all-embracing freedom, to put it poetically, while high culture stuttered its dialects fearfully and considered it noteworthy courage – that greying journalist of mine commented – if it got together with other Yugoslavs at some film or other kind of festival. There were buried mines and the remains of slaughter everywhere, everywhere apart from in my soaps, my dear. There, that's all I have to say in my defence. In short, after my series, some people took an interest in Croatian, as though it were Swahili.

Things with *Adel and Mara* didn't go quite the way they had done in the Spanish or Turkish language thanks to their own telenovellas, but they were very popular with what we might call the people, because Croatian had never been the language of imperialists and colonisers, but it still wasn't insignificant. Quite a surprise ... Kalemengo was triumphant. Without any ambition, we had achieved more for Croatian culture than the Ministry of Culture had over the previous twenty or so years. He was truly triumphant. I was awarded a medal, the president presented it to me, there's a photo. A critic in one of the daily newspapers, the same one who had coined 'orangeade', compared me to the great Croatian writer, Marija Jurić Zagorka, – he called me the serial Zagorka of our times. My saccharine passages became sentimental journeys, and pathos became the new emotionality. All at once, kitsch –always worse in the production than the script (that's all I can say in my defence) – became vitality. 'They used to jeer at Zagorka too as a writer of trash, all right not quite that, but almost, and now, look, Zagorka, hey! Imagine!' That's how the good Kalemengo put it, the fool, sweetheart. But they didn't jeer at me, although that was to be expected – apart from one single article on a feminist portal, the women journalists there really let me have it (oh yes, I realise that

they were probably right, but it's not my job to say that, my dear) –
for the most part, people praised me. For the mainstream media I
was a discovery, photogenic to boot, I say.

I admit, there were days when I thought my soap bubble works
did not have enough redeeming features. But then, with time,
I believed in all that. Besides, even those of whom it was expected
to be on a high level fell as the victims of a great general dumbing-
down. Gale, my by-then already former husband, called and said:
'Aren't you a little ashamed? Have you, perhaps, come to believe
in all that?'

'You know what they say: you can't dream, or think, or write
without dinner,' I replied.

'Who said that? Jackie Collins?'

'No.' (Virginia Woolf, in heaven's name, you clown.)

That was already the end, the end after the end. Every love has
several ends, a double or multiple lowest point. (I don't steal, I don't
stir things up, I don't pinch anyone's bread. You're no saint yourself,
you silly snob. We're all in the entertainment industry.)

'Anarchist.' (I say to Gale, and he knows that for me that means
snob.)

'In every country a decent man can only be an anarchist.' (Gale.
He's laughing.)

'But it wasn't always such a joke, or half-joke.'

Yes, it was a blow (it was), when he broke away from me with
a few ugly words (mine for the most part). I didn't feel at the time
that it was a blow, but it was. Like when I got it in the head, and the
consequences came later.

For Gale and me there was only the boat left. Our child, a shelter
for a bird and his mate. A boat that did not sail when it should have
done, to express myself poetically. He took care of it, I paid the
alimony. Methodically, into his account, with no contact if we didn't

need it. I felt good knowing that Gale had that money, some more or less regular income, I almost didn't care whether he was going to spend it on the boat or something quite else, it eased my conscience, I felt the same in connection with my mother and brother, to whom I also sent cash from time to time (but Ma died and from last year my brother is a doctor, wonderful, they don't need me any more). I had money, I didn't have time for demanding relationships.

That's how it was in Zagreb. Somewhere towards the end of recording *Adel and Mara*, I left Bert too, after seven years together. He wanted us to part ostensibly because he had discovered (I mentioned it in passing) that I had taken one of those abortion pills, that's what he called it (it was an excuse, it was a morning-after pill, that's what they're called), but I don't want to remember that, the sense of mutual contempt after a love affair is not something that should be forgotten, even hatred is better, it has some relish. And so my tom-cat Bert did not turn out to be a lion and he annulled our romanticised room-share. Now I see that was better than staying together, because in that relationship he was alone, and felt abused by inventing justifications. Apart from the early, Split phase, I remember Bert best in the form of text messages: *when are you coming? home in half an hour. Dinner's waiting, we can heat it up. I'm flying to Ljubljana this afternoon. In the bank till four then a meeting, home by eight and we can go to the cinema. morning! I'm flying to Istanbul. Catching a train to Belgrade. Driving to Graz. buy bread. l. y.* We reduced love to l. y. and death to R.I.P. (When I die, if anyone writes R.I.P., let them rot in hell!).

I missed him to start with, the light in the window as I was coming home, morning coffee before work, lying in on Sundays, naked, but the relief was greater – I was swamped with freedom. For the first time in my life, I didn't need to account to anyone, where, when, with whom, why, because there had been parents, one marriage, another – what bliss, what a blessing, freedom! Never again under the same roof with someone else, oh no, no, that isn't for me, my darling. Neither married, nor illegitimately. Together yes, but separately. (Now I know a third possibility too: solitude is sweet only when none of the household is at home, I don't like and I don't know how to be alone.)

He got married, my Bert, he had kids, he buried himself in the bank for life (which is after all a better option than having the bank bury you). There's nothing more to be said. I won't invent anything, no, I won't invent anything. Those years in Zagreb were like that, not bad: contented, on the whole, for me, always me.

Nevertheless, after the end of that second marriage, I picked up my stuff and moved to Ljubljana. So close, and yet so far, almost ideal. Anyway, if you want real success in this country, it's only possible if you move abroad. (The sun of a foreign sky gave brilliant results.) Or if you die.

At that time everyone loved me in moderation and I thank them for that. That's how I loved them too, a bit, not without sweetness. Besides, I was not in a hurry. Everything could still happen, I was only thirty-two.

But, yes, now it's the turn of this letter, the one Pironi mentioned, unusual in that it had no connection with the others, and not with the general theme either, it was even written in a different font, and there was a poem attached to it with a paper clip:

LETTER FROM A BANKER it's called

Dear Lord, who will survive, what ordinary man will not become an ordinary pauper? The problem is that the ordinary man, the fool, does not understand what is happening to him, not even an educated ordinary man who is not embedded in the system understands what is happening, because it is actually in our interests that you do not understand, that you find it all confusing, that you hope, that you wait for someone else to sort it all out. But no one will. That is why I shall explain, I shall explain and then you decide what to do. The strategy by which banks defend themselves is logical, but also transparent. It can all be seen, for example, in the way in which we would resolve problems of loans in Swiss francs. So, we help existentially threatened debtors, the most desperate of the desperate, but not all of them, as they include also rogues who have bought a second or a third property. If you know anything you will see at once that with this proposal we are breaking one of the main rules of our financial trade: the one that says that banks are not social institutions. Where would it lead if banks started granting exemptions for debts because of their debtors' financial and existential problems? Who would ever pay their instalments in full, if it was possible to negotiate and bargain with a bank? But nevertheless, banks suddenly believe tears. Why?

Evidently, in order to avoid the question that goes: are our rates extortionate and what is our business practice like in general? We bankers are ready to acknowledge the difficulties in which our debtors have found themselves, but heaven forbid that it should occur to anyone that the blame lies with us or with the system that we ourselves devised. Our strategy amounts to a typical replacement of the thesis. It's all about a crisis and poverty, and not about us. Such humanism might, to be honest, cost us some money, but that is quite unlikely, negligible. When people start demonstrating their personal misery or the worth or the profitability of some inherited real estate or a holiday home from happier days, then one comes back to that question from the psalm: Who, oh Lord, will survive?

Who will survive, ladies and gentlemen, comrades?

Did we tell you that no other way is possible? Remember, little Iceland (population 329 thousand), which was until its crisis a paradise for foreign banks, recovered. In an interview, their president said: 'We were warned that we would become the Cuba of the north if we did not sanitise our banks.' It all turned out to be false. That is to say, Iceland did not advocate the replacement of the thesis, perhaps because there are more rogues there who believe that they have deserved more from life than a roof and bread, and, there, the state saved the thrifty and left the banks to be saved by their owners or to fail. The result was that a country that seven years earlier had been on the brink of bankruptcy today has a faster rate of economic growth than America or Great Britain (which are more successful in the so-called western world), and unemployment was significantly reduced. This makes them twice as good as the European average. 'We refused to spend state funds to cover the losses of private banks,' says the president of Iceland. 'We were exposed to unbelievable political and economic pressure to follow the orthodox doctrines to which all European governments and financial institutions adhere, and which have proved economically, democratically, politically and judicially erroneous.' The president of Iceland does not mention judicially by chance. The Icelanders even took the directors of their banks to court.

It is said that politicians want to subordinate the banks, which must have sufficient profits to repay their shareholders' investments, even when they cannot refund loans, which is the favourite replacement thesis. One ought thus to conclude that what is being questioned is normal banking business and not the practice of Croatian banks. Banks are commercial entities, which, like other merchants, sell their products on the market … say the bankers, explaining that the state should not interfere. But this is bullshit, notably: long ago the banks in Croatia formed cartels and so suspended the market, which neither the state nor its institutions opposed. What is more, it worked for them, above all through hard-currency stipulation and relinquishing monetary sovereignty. After that they and their foreign masters simply could no longer stop themselves grabbing everything life offered them. That is how we came to be in a situation in which a large proportion of the nation lives in debtors' slavery, and the interest charged is such that there is no legitimate work from whose income it would be possible to pay it. In fact, the national economy is in hock to the banks. It sounds good when the prime minister – so it says in the papers – at last replies to the banks, which are threatening international disputes, that they should sue him. But for a real solution it is necessary.

TO BLOW UP THE BANKS
Should the banks be blown up?
Yes, yes, one should roll up one's sleeves
Turn up one's collar
Go out into the street on a wonderful warm night

Vanish into the crowd
Let off fireworks
Or even just stay in that street
With the lit-up faces and ordinary smiles
Of a hero and heroine
Waiting to be taken away
So, should one then blow up the banks?
Yes, yes, one should
In the night while there are no people
Only the precise bureaucratic and disinfected
Soul of the house
Fill this empty moneybag with a boom
A merry boom created
From the silent hardship of millions
From a string of tragedies that are growing
To a spectacular explosion
Should those churches of today's life, with god fragmented into
small coins,
What are you saying, be destroyed to their foundations?
Yes, yes, they should
There's no doubt
Burn banknotes
Fill the summer town
With the stench of petrol
With a wild fire in which what will vanish first
Are the index cards and old newspapers of your humiliation.
That flame will quickly devour
Our expendable blood
Blood for drunken fat cats' cocktail parasols
Don't be afraid (there won't be any blood apart perhaps from ours)
Don't wait (the right moment is now)

Go out naked, in pyjamas and slippers
Wait for me by the cash machine
It will be the first to get its comeuppance
We will be lit up by an unprecedented gleam
You will see how wondrous is the flaming face
Of forgotten justice
It is dangerous, it is simple, it is unsatisfied
And just around the corner

This imaginary Banker comes from a bank-noir, an ordinary former boy, today a manager, but never the top one (the top ones don't live in Dinko Šimunović Street, Nightingale knows that). The banker was woken in the night by the dirty little games in the neighbourhood or maybe he suffers from insomnia because of all those numbers, succeeding one another behind his eyelids, and he thought: this is what should be done, this is how priorities should be laid out. (In a moment of lucidity, he probably thought like that, but quickly set it aside, because what about his wife, what about his children? Who would buy them meat and milk, or Stracciatella ice-cream? And I am only a small cog, at best a rear wheel in that machine that crushes houses, dreams, corpses – that's what he thinks – and I am easily replaced by another.)

But, let's say the banker does not have a wife and children on his back, only his career, like Bert, but he boils over, and, inspired by the wave of letters, he sits down and writes this letter of his to his neighbours, distributes it surreptitiously, like a cuckoo its eggs. He must at least write an anonymous letter, that'll save him for a while, he'll feel better, and, if he's lucky, the worm of doubt might stop niggling at him by the end of his holiday. But why leave it at that, if we're already imagining things …

For the last few days, life has looked like this: after the morning when I help Arrow and Billy Goat (now I really can help) with the animals and preparing food, comes the afternoon when we climb into the forest to the well for water (the summer was hot and there is just a little ice-cold water in the depths of the well, and sometimes we draw up a live frog in the bucket), then, as soon as the sun turns pink in the west, they take me to Gramps and Granma's house, swaying on the top of the hill, beside the weather station, still a little charred from the war and as though askew on the downward slope. The thirteen-year-old chamois scamper from bush to bush, while I patter after them in a pair of Helanka's galoshes they've lent me. (What kind of footwear is this, maybe she wears them to clean the stable.)

I hardly dare even think of who they look like to me, but they mostly remind me of my mum, although that is not a straightforward thought. (Their faces are an agreeable, perhaps even an astonishing sight: Helanka's face was an event, Helanka had no eyebrows, she had no eyelashes, generally she had always possessed a complete lack of downiness. When she was a little girl in a small town, those features had caused her problems, but her interesting body richly compensated for that sacrifice when she grew up and set off into the world.

Along the way, we pick edible, inedible and poisonous things, let me learn: hellebore, raspberries, wild peas that grow hidden in the corn, dog mushrooms (they grow out of dog shit, of course) and green hazelnuts, bitter, with still soft skins. When we pass rosemary, they say: 'Stroke the rosemary, then sniff your hands and you'll get better' (among other things, rosemary strengthens the memory, restores recollections, not when you ingest it, only when you smell it and release the smell by stroking it.)

After grazing, the girls are followed into the barn by ten snowy sheep and two well-fed cows (with their eyes and rear ends full of flies), Lily Allen and Goldie, they check the hen coop, then beside the coop set off through the high uncut grass, as high as my neck – and up to their ears – but they are not afraid of snakes, neither mines nor snakes, they know the way. The flowers have gone crazy. Billy Goat scurries about with her bill-hook, Arrow, dark, with her long stride, waves her little axe. (We two sisters are waging war, do not weep, mother, if we should perish.)

Then from the top of the hill down a grassy slope a white-haired man with a moustache calls,

'Who's this coming? Grandpa's treasures,' and that voice rolls down to us and draws us uphill. We reach a little house, the home of the Golubić family: Gramps, Granma and their son Jusuf (poor Jusuf).

The sight I saw on one wall of the hay-loft, as soon as I had climbed up and stood in front of the house, moved me: the Mona Lisa painted on the wall and people with desperate expressions on their faces (people and their children) clutching at her skirts, her décolleté and soft skin, beneath her lips. They gush out of the frame of the picture, wanting to be embraced, to be saved by a Mona Lisa. It was not the subject matter that moved me, I had seen more terrible things on the same theme (paintings of drowning people wash over the world of the indifferent). But I was shaken by the fact that Nightingale had been here (I placed my feet where his feet had stood while he drew the Giaconda's lips). I laid my cheek and part of my nose against her smooth, cold décolleté. From that angle, when I opened my eyes, my attention was drawn to a small washed (scratched?) cartoon cloud over the Mona Lisa's head, one of those with little bubbles rising from the head, suggesting thoughts. When you went closer, you could make out that what was written on them was: Muslims!

'I don't know how to read this script. Is it true that imps write?'

'I wouldn't call them imps, Gramps. They're refugees.'

'The devil who drew that said that imps wrote, God guide him away to the woods. As for those refugees. Oh, what a crazy world, dear people.'

'Can I ask you something, was the man who drew this called Nightingale?'

'Nightingale? I don't know anything, nothing, I swear. A lad came before dawn, I had just got up to go to the toilet, he asked me politely if he could paint the wall. And why not – I hadn't expected that. He sauntered around, then left, he didn't even have coffee – I had made it for him. Granma woke up late, complained a bit, but calmed down when she recognised the Virgin. Come on, let's go inside, don't stand in a draught!'

'That's not what it represents.' I wanted to explain.

'I know it's not, devil take it.'

'Can I ask you something: has a man called Nightingale been here? Fairish hair (he may have gone a bit grey, I haven't seen him for a long time), light eyes, neither tall nor short, roughly my height, slim, with a strong torso.'

'What about his legs?'

'Bandy, thin. If he hasn't put on weight.'

'Why are legs crucial. Heavens.'

'And his hands?'

'Working hands, dear. Although he's not a worker in the usual sense. Un-cared for, let's say. Hands bigger than his face!'

'And his teeth?'

'You're kidding me. Good teeth. A very charming smile.'

'No.'

'There's not been anyone like that.'

'People come here only with off-road vehicles. You're the first in a convertible. Has he got an off-road vehicle?'

'I don't know. I don't think he can drive.'

'And does he work in healthy foods?'

'I don't believe he has anything to do with that sort of thing, dear, he's an artist. He draws, writes, graffiti, poems, performance art.'

'Huh, we're more into film, Arrow and me, (Laughter.) And what is he? A lovebird?'

'Lover, you mean.'

'Former husband. But there's something I need, that's important to me.'

'Ho-ho, secrets!'

'Mysterious.'

'Not exactly mysterious, intimate. A diary.'

'Ho-ho, intimate secrets!'

'We saw you in the papers last year. Mum said you're going to die.'

'Good heavens, Arrow. She either torments you or she shoots you! Mum was very sad.'

'I'm not dead, I had a car crash, but look at me, I survived. It's not too clever to believe the papers, dear.'

'Yes, you're definitively alive. But we don't know that guy.'

'I do.'

'You don't, Arrow.'

'I do, Billy, Mitar. That's him.'

'No it's not. Could he be? I'm glad you're alive.'

'Yees. Mitar, our little friend. Painter. Artist.'

'Wow, he's your husband! Why, he's made lots of pictures here. He came several times. And in Split, too. There are some of his in the Red School. Murals. He used a hundred sprays and paints and then one day he wasn't there anymore. But we don't know where he went to, maybe Mum knows.'

'You came back to life and you're looking for your former husband.'

'You could put it like that, my dear Arrow, you could.'

'I'm not really into romance.'

'You're more into Jusuf.'

'That's not funny.'

(In the evening, through the blue and mauve, Jusuf sometimes steals up, bringing wild mushrooms, he doesn't say anything, just 'hello'. We cook them in milk or fry them on a bare ring with bacon, for supper.)

I can't tell them, those children (a blue and mauve evening has gathered outside, and crickets can be heard, along with an animal rooting round the house), but I can say it to myself, in the manner of the queen of soap opera: Those letters did bring me back to life. I would like to drive the whole night through to find him, I would like to run for miles towards him, swim for miles, like before, if I knew where he was. Although we haven't seen each other for years, the fact that he is inaccessible is driving me to despair.

Sooner or later the crass question arises: is this all there is? Up to now I have lived life without being in love. Now I know, you have to come and ask shamelessly of the one you fall for: give me our love. If he has it, he'll give it, in time. If he hasn't, you have nothing to lose, it's already lost. You have to be persistent in your attention, your adoration, to seduce and captivate, most people fall in love with someone's love, certainly more than with someone's legs (so we've heard). You need to invest everything in order to gain something (all or nothing!) in this field of emotion. This is not a dress-rehearsal for real life, no, no, it's all a first night. And love is the only genuine spectacle on offer, if you don't like war. If love is secondary, then everything is secondary. If love is not important, then there is nothing serious between birth and death, apart from serious illness. So what? I think there is a possibility that we take love for granted, like something natural, that goes without saying, with no pomp, but that is just cynical and boring and desperate, that world in which love, if there is any, is strictly private, in which loves are not impermissible, and they are all put in the cupboard, while the greatest erotic excitement is approached with recipes, stirring liquids in a glass and today's menu.

LETTER FROM AN INCURABLE WOMAN PATIENT

You erotic monsters,

I am in no doubt that you would find it strange if you were only aware of how your *squealing sex acts*, your wild cries and idiotic behaviour have made my life interesting again, when I had already felt for years that I had had enough. Of course, I've had enough only of suffering, there's never enough of life. To start with you irritated and disgusted me, then you bothered me – I wanted to sleep –(but I can't sleep anyway) then I found you comical, then my body briefly forgot its pain and sent me a mild signal of excitement, perhaps an intimation of pleasure, then a clear memory of pleasure, a desire for touch and finally a touch. I thought about carnal love, about that animal-like thing between you, between us, animal in a nice way, about something I had in my early youth, but then I didn't know how vehemently and greedily I ought to have snatched that life, because it would vanish, unnoticed, like *white on white*, like *water in water*. And I wanted to be vulgar, indecent, excessive. I wanted to erupt and forget my thoughts and my head and my limbs. Now I'm no longer afraid, I would know how to abandon myself and I would not ask the price. Illness has prepared me for love, but both are incurable.

Although I know I shall not recover, if I ever should recover I shall
(pamper my body like this):
Make love up in the air on the highest floor, on top of the town,
among the clouds.

Although I know I shall not recover, if I ever should recover I shall:
Make love in a forest in the embrace of a man and a tree trunk.

Although I know I shall not recover, if I ever should recover I shall:
Make love in a boat on the open sea.

Although I know I shall not recover, if I ever should recover I shall:
Make love with a beautiful, intelligent woman with a pleasant voice.

Although I know I shall not recover, if I ever should recover I shall:
Make love with a good, strong young man with dark skin and a huge
member.

Although I know I shall not recover, if I ever should recover I shall:
Make love in the sea.

Although I know I shall not recover, if I ever should recover I shall:
Make love with someone doing it for the first time.

Although I know I shall not recover, if I ever should recover I shall:
Make love on the kitchen table.

Although I know I shall not recover, if I ever should recover I shall:
Make love more often in the 69 position.

Although I know I shall not recover, if I ever should recover I shall:
Have more important obligations than
To make love every day with the one I love every day.

Billy Goat, long-legged, boyish, slender, gambols with her bill-hook. Arrow, almost the same, radiant, pink, stern, with shining eyes, long-legged and light-footed, lopes about with her small axe; they have rucksacks on their backs. They are as light as though strolling through Manhattan. Arrow usually has headphones from which a drum throbs into the mountain silence. Because of the clarity of the air, seen from the valley where Helanka's farm sits, the hill looks as close as after rain, but it takes nearly an hour to reach the top on foot. But there is no other way and this slow pace relaxes me. Some things cannot be done quickly: walking, conquering a hill, reading a book, listening to music, sleeping and so on. This could be a refuge, this could be plan B. It's a shame that I have so loved towns all my life, their streets and harbours and urban wildness and people brought up in those laboratory conditions of rooms, squares, clubs. I do know a little about the natural world thanks to growing up by the sea. This wildness suits me now. In this empty space in which traces of humans are erased, which nature has reclaimed anew as at the beginning of the world.

When I'm walking with the young girls, I myself am a girl. Nature is big and mystical, while we are wild beasts of forest and field. A wayward ranger and two swift highway-women. After we pass the half-way point, then, from the top of the hill, down the grassy slope a white-haired moustached man bellows: 'Who's this coming, Grandpa's treasures,' and that voice reverberates round the whole valley. Then, when we come quite close to the slanting plateau where the family's house sits askew, the big-eared grandfather puts his fingers in his mouth and whistles. The sisters laugh. Billy Goat giggles. Arrow smiles and rolls her eyes.

Near the house, some twenty metres above it, on the very top, is the weather station, automatic. Gramps keeps an eye on it, maintains it, especially in winter when it ices up, that is his job, he checks the sensors that resemble his own fleshy ears. It is from the station that Billy Goat and Arrow are able to steal the satellite signal (in their rucksacks are tablets slimmer than a bar of chocolate or a mirror).

Gramps is speaking. 'The day will come when technology will outgrow international relations. We'll get a generation of idiots, said Einstein. And here I am, I'm that idiot. I don't even speak to my wife and son, but I'm forever chattering to these sensors. Dear God if Tejica and Mejri here didn't come to see me I'd never speak to a human being.'

'Tea and Meri, Gramps, without the 'j'.' They correct him for using the diminutive, but they're not looking at him any more, they are already absorbed.

Then another old voice is heard beyond the half-closed door. 'Little sluts, they've come for grandpa to poke then on the manure heap behind the barn, to stick them on his great cock, to quarter them. The old man has a huge dick, he sticks it in the hens and they die, he sticks it in the cow's cunt, the mare, the bitch and the donkey's hole, and offers his hole to the horse. If he shoves his dick into your little fannies, you'll be done for, little tarts, its head will come out of your mouths. Better let the old man lick you with his ox's tongue than impale you on his cock. Better rub yourselves with straw than let him put his ram's trotter into your cunt.'

'Oh, that's Granma!' Billy Goat signals that the old woman is mad.

(I am so flabbergasted that perhaps for the first time I understand the meaning of the word flabbergasted.)

Grandpa is mortified. 'I'm so sorry, madam, what a disgrace, dear Lord … She wasn't always like that. Now, for some time, she's been this way, she goes crazy, out of the blue, throws her pills away, refuses to take them, and says loathsome things, oh my dear Lord … If I'd known that you were coming this evening, I would have locked her up.' He winks.

I stand still, I don't know what to say. And out of the house comes the owner of the voice, a little old lady with thin lips, probably toothless, in a dark old-fashioned dress and a blue scarf on her head. Granma.

'Where you from?'

'From Split,' I say.

'A Croat then, fuck it. No matter, the main thing is you're not a heathen. I've had enough of them under my roof. You got children?'

'No,' I say.

'Why, in god's name? Barren, of course. Never mind. It's better not to have kids, any cur is better than one's own son. You feed him, take the food from your own mouth, and he converts, becomes a Turk. That fart, my son, fuck his father, is a Turk. And he's not snipped! One morning I find him with a bare bum, groaning, he's fucking a hole in the ground. Found a mole and stuck it on his cock blindly, and it's shrieking. Another time he screwed a tree in a wasp nest and a badger in the mouth, for god's sake, and paid for it. The badger pruned his cock for him! And he bonks these girls, and their mother, in the trough. Look at them, just see her elbows, in heaven's name! Scabbed! From screwing on the ground.'

At this Billy Goat shouted: 'I fell off the mule chasing a sheep, that naughty one, are you crazy?! Tell her! Gramps!'

Grandpa said: 'Gran, please, go inside, get into the house! Or I'll take the whip to you!'

Here the obscene old woman scurried over the threshold and ran into the house. And the old man, her minder, smiled as though nothing had happened (he waved his stick, chasing an invisible fly), as though a child had sworn. He invited us to sit on a bench on the veranda: 'Here, sit and rest.'

He's completely white, the old man they call Gramps, covered in thick white fur out of which the deep furrows of his face peer, he has knots and lumps of hands, but youthful gestures. For instance, when he lifts his foot onto a tree stump or fence, and lays his hands on his knee with his chin in his palm to consider or examine something. Then he does not look like Heidi's grandpa: in that pose he is like a thoughtful boy or a feminist in the first half of last century. Not exactly an everyday scene and it soothes me.

The girls were surfing single-mindedly, entranced, while I, in the absence of a stronger drug, hit the juniper brandy in an attempt to cleanse the old woman, and the whip, from my head. The next morning (which is today) I had forgotten how to drive, probably forever.

I had silicon lips and perfectly whitened teeth, I had a Brazilian hairstyle, good, expensive clothes, I drove a golden two-seater, a Mazda convertible, similar to the one I drive now, and my hair is golden blond and my veneer is still shiny, but I am a black orange, opaque inside. Empty, ever emptier, full of hell.

It began with the alphabet, at first I had difficulty writing. It was a consequence of the car crash that happened a bit more than a year ago on my way into Zagreb. The newspapers wrote extensively about my condition, thirstily waiting for racy news of my death, which would sell out their entire print-run. I had already been mourned on several portals, gateways to the future. Someone, evidently upset, announced it first, and then others carried the news that spread like wildfire. It was no longer possible to stop it. (Poor Kalemengo, he got very irritated by the phone calls.) If I had been despised alive, I was adored dead. It's a shame it only lasted a few hours, and then in the main News people apologised to me (who, in that dynamic time of my false death, was entirely out of it, I hardly existed) and to my family (consisting of my brother).

My little brother (whom I rarely saw because of my commitments), already by then an intern in a hospital, a recently qualified doctor (nevertheless, let it be noted, as I am already recording, I paid for his education) took me under his wing, I was examined by the best surgeons and neurosurgeons. Both my arms were broken, two ribs and most of my teeth. I had serious concussion. I almost lost an eye. They patched me and cobbled me together again, you can notice it, and I can feel it.

Waking from a short-lived coma, after a month, I came home, to my brother's care. The media spread the news of my miraculous recovery, but they did not all cover my return to life with equal zeal, with fireworks, the way they had announced my death, so some people still thought I was dead and some that I was dying. I thought I was recovering.

Everything had apparently got back to normal, after several operations. I travelled to Ljubljana, back to my life, to my colleagues and friends, to the life I had set up, established as firmly as I could, my dear. I had enough money, that could buy me security, happiness, even health, new teeth, new car, new parts for me. Money can do lots, people lie. Although some things, of course, it can't, my dear. I waited for Gale to get in touch, as always when something happened. And he would without fail send a message (after our last quarrel, ten years ago, he no longer called, he just sent text messages that were always a shock, like a gentle blow to the stomach). He sent them every week,

then every month,

then when he had some reason,

and that was twice: my divorce (about which the media talked the usual garbage), my mother's death (he saw the announcement) and once for no reason

He would ask how I was.

I'm fine, thanks, hanging in there, how are you.

OK, same as ever.

Take care.

And you.

This time he did not contact me. He let me die. I wanted to call him and say: 'Hey, I died, and not a word from you.' (Black tongue, black noon, black hope to you. Everything black, only may my horror be white.)

He was not in Split any more then, probably not in Croatia. (Is he in Europe at all? Is he alive, dear?)

I was soon taken up with other things. First I forgot where the letters on keyboards were, my fingers forgot their practised moves. I stopped sending messages, I stopped writing, it took too much effort, the doctor said I should try slowly, gradually. I now find it harder even to read, probably because of a lack of concentration, but I can do it. To start with letters slipped away from me, they changed places, and later I could not even recall the symbols. They weren't sure (in the hospital) what was going on, an X-ray showed some damage, clouds, lakes, lesions: my brain is now a moon with the moon's seas (the Sea of Tranquillity, the Ocean of Storms …). Into these spaces of emptiness all my unwritten words and the alphabet vanished, all thirty symbols in infinite permutations, leaving me only entirely disconnected ones.

Sometimes I would fantasise about stopping writing. (Not like this, in this way.) For a while I wrote that poetry about which I have no opinion and which I have not kept: everyone has always scribbled something. (It vanished somewhere with my old note-books and school exercise books when Ma and my brother moved away to one place, and I to another.) Still, I recall a certain sense of liberation when I gave up poetry forever. I began to think and live in a different way. I didn't need to be anything for twenty-four hours a day, let alone a poet, and writing is what it does for people, it takes possession of them, stops them from living. One day I woke up (let's say) and I could do whatever I wanted, because I wasn't thinking about writing any more. It's different with scripts, there the characters take over your thoughts, why they're paper hordes, man. For most of my free time, I thought about them, the characters, their actions, what they thought about, why they were the way they were and what was going to happen to them. There wasn't much space for real people. Even on holiday, on journeys, at a pleasant dinner and even in bed I caught myself making a story out of little fragments of life, unable to leave anything be, let myself go and simply live. Who would not wish to rest from that, forever. At that time, one of the actresses, nice and talented, of a loving nature (she changed partners frequently and those relationships were stormy) told me that she could hardly wait for her libido to dry up.

'How do you mean dry up?!'

'It is annoying me,' said the actress, 'sexual desire doesn't let me live calmly and reflect, it gets in my way and makes problems for me.'

What happened to me with writing came from the same or a neighbouring gland.

'Lots of people would like to lose their heads,' I told her, 'but it never happens to them. Try to think of it as a gift.'

But I was wrong, people don't at all want to lose their heads, people are like me and her, they wish, in the name of peace or in the name of self-control, to lose their gift. Are not some things mistakenly called the joy of life? Perhaps there's no comparison, but my brother complained that his patients (women, for the most part), if they're prescribed Prozac for depression, want Normabel. Prozac doesn't suit them at all, they rebel. They don't want to be happier, they just want to sleep through it all and be done with it.

After a careful diagnosis that seriously presupposed the possibility that similar things would happen to me, that this would not be confined to dysgraphia and that my condition of forgetting was progressive (they didn't find a name for my condition, although they offered several baleful names), I sold my possessions: the renovated flat in Zagreb in which I had once lived with Bert (two rooms), a little holiday house on the Kornati island Žut, which I rarely visited (my first major, romantic investment), my golf kit (my most recent and stupidest investment), everything apart from my clothes, the Ljubljana bachelor pad and Woody Mary. I had no intention of selling Woody Mary, as I had told Pironi in Split, but of making her over to Gale. (I had carefully planned how to do this, my dear, so that it did not look magnanimous or ostentatious, but necessary and the only correct thing to do.) I fantasied about that meeting, waited for better arguments and, here, the time has come when I have to give in.

Not long after I had sold everything, quickly and for a decent price, I was visited by an unknown nocturnal guest. He knew whose place he had come to and what he wanted. He asked for money, he was quiet, but I wasn't asleep. He was a dark shadow, but his voice was young. When he saw that I had sat up, then covered my face, he squatted beside my bed and spoke these two sentences: 'I won't hurt you, you needn't be afraid, give me cash and I'm off. You're dying, you don't need money any more, but I do.' He won't hurt me. One of the uninitiated. I'm not dying, dear, only I shall soon forget everything, that's how things are, that's what I wanted to say, but I didn't. I saw the whites of his eyes in the darkness and his bare arms hanging relaxed by his sides. I got out of bed, carefully (I'm afraid of being hurt), opened my drawer and placed the money in front of him, a lot of money, everything I had not lodged in my bank account. He was young, yes, and as far as could be made out, ugly and skinny, when I approached him, he trembled. (From fear?) He grabbed my arms, presumably so that I couldn't hit him with anything, although I would not have been in a position to. We were both afraid (I think) and watched each other in that fear. I don't think he had much experience of robbery, as far as I could see, he didn't have any weapons at all.

I liked spending money. I didn't need it, no, I didn't need it in fact, because I had it, and now I needed less and less. I say: 'I won't switch on the alarm when you leave, I won't scream, I won't telephone, I just want you to stay with me a bit longer.'

'What are you afraid of? Thieves?'

'I'm afraid of being on my own,' I say, 'not usually but now, just recently.'

It was spoken very intimately, as though I had at that moment leapt over miles to reach this pathetic creature. I touched the crook of his arm, then his shoulder. He made a movement, roughly, to stop me, but then as though he had twigged, he kissed me. He put both his hands on my backside, which made me laugh and relaxed me (a child, a virgin), and shoved his nose forcefully into my neck, beside my ear, sniffing doggedly.

One could say I seduced him, induced him, that kid, that crook, probably an addict. I did it, it's easy when you decide to, it was just a moment. I didn't undress him, I felt the smell of sweat and deodorant, I sat him on the bed and unzipped him, slipped a condom onto him (a good habit, my dear), settled on to him and twitched a few times, holding him firmly pressed against my body as though he meant something to me. After the boy came (quickly), he hastily did up his trousers. He tossed a few big banknotes onto the table and fled. It came to him, poor lad, he paid me with my own money. It's not easy to be a man, toting so much pride around. There's so much ego, and so little dignity in this world, sweetheart. In fact, it's a question of style, I thought, lighting a cigarette.

Jusuf drove me to the Red School, over the fields, he didn't want to take any money.

I had woken before dawn, white and chilly, and listened from my bed to a bird. It was singing somewhere in the maize. A lovely song, but it wasn't a nightingale. They sing at night, but also during the day, if no one disturbs them. In this region, nightingales sing for just a month or two in the spring, then calm down, at this time of year they have probably flown off somewhere, to Africa presumably, my dear. Here the sky is wide open, as it is for instance above the sea, open as a cupola and right up until dawn you can see millions of stars advancing into the darkness and gloom. In towns the sky is staged differently, there is less sky, it's shallower, in some towns there is none at all for months, people live seriously, on the earth. (The lives of moles look very serious to moles like us.)

As I felt cold in the morning, I pulled my writing clothes on where I was, under the cover. It's not an extravagant, unwearable outfit; it's very comfortable, reminiscent of Japanese costumes, with a short, folding upper part and soft, comfortable slacks. On one side black, and on the other white. I put them on, white side out. It's a bit baggy on me, this outfit of yours, Gale. Baggy, but short. Do you remember when I told you that I loved you because you were so rare, a man with a woman's heart, and you replied that every nightingale was once Philomena, a captive woman whose tongue had been cut out. 'Do you hear, do you hear me, are you a nightingale?' I shouted to the night bird (I think it was a blackbird) under the window, under the Milky Way, in the maize that had just ripened. But what could the damn bird reply?

I sing the way a bird sings
Living on a branch
The song that bursts through my throat
Rewards me abundantly.

I remembered those lines (they were great for annoying Gale), as I did many other poems, even also some striking sections of several philosophical tracts, cake recipes, mathematical formulae, the titles of most of the romances I had read and written, but after so many years of driving I no longer knew how to start a car. I didn't tell anyone that yesterday, when I wanted to move it into the shed, that I couldn't start the car. I said, later, my dear, that I had twisted my wrist so I couldn't drive (I lay down in the grass beside the convertible and tried to pull myself together, to summon the movements one by one as though I was learning them for the first time).

Jusuf. Morning. He knocked, fragrant, his hair combed, but still sulky, because a wild dog crouches in him. 'I hear you need a driver?'

He doesn't ask why.

'I'm coming, I'm coming,' I say.

I tied a silk scarf round my hair and went out. And then I went back inside, took off the galoshes and put on high heels, I mustn't sell myself short, otherwise, if you let yourself go, everything can so easily go downhill, my mother used to say when things were at their most difficult for her, and it's not a bad recipe, and simple adherence to a recipe sometimes suits me. Besides, Jusuf is not attractive. That does not remotely mean that I want to seduce him – but yes, I want to look good, not at any price or above all, but as long as I please people I'm alive. It's a passive eroticism, self-eroticism, on the whole a female thing – a coquette, narcissist, performer, looks at her reflection in all shop windows, adjusts her make-up in every rear-view mirror and feels a joyfulness and a mostly unconscious erotic excitement which for the most part does not seek to be expressed – although very handsome men can escape it with difficulty, not to mention transvestites. (The other person is on the whole only a mirror.) That mistakenly interpreted behaviour, which represents either harmless pleasure in oneself or a very professional, subtle work on charisma (I've seen plenty of that among actresses, but also actors!), although it stems from a deeply secret source of sexuality, is more virginal than whoreish. But if it were the other way round – so what?

Here are a few things about Jusuf which I managed to glean because he's not talkative, my dear. Jusuf, the real one, was the father of his classmate, a policeman, who was killed at the start of the war by the fathers of other classmates. That was while he (this present one, our Jusuf) was living in town with his older sister. The town has been virtually wiped out, after the war few returned, some new people moved in, just a few of them, not enough to stop the town gaping like a mouth of broken teeth. It was settled largely by Croats, also from devastated villages, but it was hard to live with them. All that remained of the Orthodox and Muslim families that had lived there before were their graves. First the Serbs chased the Muslims out, and then the Croats the Serbs. There was nothing about that on the News, ever, not on anyone's news.

'And the sister? The sister is in Canada.'

'Clearing snow?'

'Cleaning houses.'

Srđan, the son of the weather-watcher Gramps and crazy Granma, whom his parents hid in the cellar so that he wouldn't be taken off to war (he had just reached the best age for war!), went to an office where you go for such things, filled in some forms and changed his name to Jusuf.

Well Foucault supported Khomeini, I think. Chomsky, Pol Pot. Heidegger, Hitler. Really discouraging. A lot of humanism distances you from people, sometimes big ideas can disorient a person.

'Fool,' Gramps told him, 'you bloody fool, that's not the way to do things.' (His father didn't support Jusuf.)

'Why not, why, so many people changed their first names and surnames in the war, I can do that in peacetime,' that's what Jusuf said (he said it and laughed). He didn't want oblivion. He didn't want escape. Disagreeable Jusuf appeals to me, one of the spat-upon, despised by everyone, a revolutionary of a quiet, solitary revolution, with no bullet fired, with no parade (with no justice).

'Others are no better, my dear,' I told Jusuf, 'just look at what they've done to your village, you wouldn't know it had ever existed.'

Jusuf said: 'That's what my father says, that people are not rice grains – all alike,' he consoles himself that ours were the worst (like hell), even worse than the gypsies who exterminated them round here. Who on earth would come back when all the old folk, the whole village, died in concentration camps? As though they had been plucked out of the earth. 'What did he go back to the forest for? Fuck it all,' he said of his father. 'I'd like to set fire again with my own hands to him and my mother and the house and that weather station! Let people kill each other, fuck them all, I'm not even sorry for the children, in five, ten or fifty years they'll be raping and slaughtering too. Everything should be set on fire and razed like this village, the whole of the Balkans, let it all be covered over with grass and then everything can start again afresh.'

'Listen to the maestro, he'd flatten it all. You're a positive thinker, sweetheart, you mustn't think like that. To say all people are evil is as stupid as saying they're all good. It plays into the devil's hands.'

'What devil's that?'

'Metaphorical. Of course.'

I didn't say anything else. And he stopped talking about it too, black as he was, he just bristled even more and sunk his head between his shoulders.

The vehicle swayed slowly over flowers and grass, stones and mole-hills. 'Grand little car,' said the driver. 'A shame to take it over this terrain.'

It (the car) reminded me of me, pricking my way in my high heels over the fields and meadows, and I thought it must look comical.

We noticed that someone was following us through the tall grasses, someone grown up with blades of grass, hiding in the rocky hollows and among the maize stalks, in the corn, yellow and green like the corn.

Jusuf was angry. 'The leech, the little leech. I'll end up in jail because of that girl, I'll have to inform her mother,' said Jusuf (angrily) following the slender figure moving in the rear-view mirror. Arrow.

'Are you sleeping with her?'

'With the girl?! Wash your mouth out.'

'Why no, in heaven's name, with Helanka?'

'No. And what exactly does it have to do with you?'

'My dear, you're not going to tell me that you came to this village which is never going to be renovated in order to mend the sensors on the weather station with your daddy or to listen to your mother going crazy.'

He said: 'She has days, mother, when she forgets her medication, she's not always, she doesn't swear ... Oh, forget it.'

'You've fallen in love. I'm an expert in these things. A theorist,' I say.

'I haven't the cash, my friend, to even think of love. There's no love in my pay grade. But there's cream, there are apples, blueberries, eggs, honey, wool, potatoes, plums, mushrooms, everything. I distribute it all around, I drive, I help at the ranch, the woman gave me work: the old girl wanted a devil but bought a pig. Listen, I fell for her, but I'm not a child. What good would I be rotting in an office in town or maybe collecting empty bottles?'

'Why aren't you doing the distribution now, my dear? The boss has gone herself?'

'We quarrelled. She's got a husband.'

'In Split, I know,' I say. 'Danny-Boy, he was a DJ, now he's into mobile phones. He's got shops. He sells mobiles and mends them.'

'Well, there, good luck to him, she lives with him there, and with me here. He knows about it.'

'Hmmm,' I say.

'Like Tilda Swinton.'

'Who?' I say.

'Like the actress.'

'Yes, I know, my dear, but Tilda lives with both of them, her husband and her lover, under the same roof, that's what I've read,' I say. 'That's not the same as your set-up. You don't know him, but it's hard to believe that Helanka married Danny-Boy, a real Split show-off. Why did you quarrel, because she's got a husband? You must like her since you're with her.'

'Like her? Nothing wrong with her, I don't dislike her. This isn't Hollywood. Here you don't even notice the smell of shit any more. And somehow one has to live until death. Shift your arse, sister. We're here.'

'This poet of yours, the artist, I got to know him when he came here. A regular guy, but very interesting.'

'What do you want to know, Jusuf?'

'Why are you looking for him after so many years?'

'Because I still love him, sweetheart,' I say.

'Why?'

'My brain is failing. There's something wrong with me, it came on after a car crash, not at once, later. My brain fails, I forget things.'

'Your actual life's like a soap opera, then.'

'There, you see. I've forgotten how to write, in a few months, or days, or hours, I'll forget how to read, or how to eat, or why to use the toilet. To drive. There, sweetheart.'

'Would it help you? To find that man,' Jusuf asked.

I'm disappearing, I thought, but I didn't say that.

I said that yes, it would certainly help me. 'He left letters before he went away, they're not exactly addressed to me, but they were left for me. When I read them, I hear his voice, that's the voice of my young husband,' I say. 'And ever since I read the letters, maybe even before that, I decided to find him.' (I'm not asking for anything. I'm no longer grasping, or poor, or ambitious.) 'We were fantastic together, so young and head-over-heels, it was fireworks, my dear. And we knew that we were happy and that we were alive. Do you feel alive? It didn't stop us breaking each other's hearts, but when did it?' I say.

'When indeed,' Jusuf confirmed.

'Today I don't have anything of his from those days, maybe a photograph,' I say. 'I don't think that I should have stayed in the same place with him, I did what I needed to do. But, as is often the way – the reasons why we're not together have long since ceased to be important, while the reasons why we were together have endured. Our reasons still exist today, just as beautiful, clear and irrefutable. When I catch that lost emotion, rapture, I could run all over this hill without stopping. And now I'm supposed to forget what it is that keeps my head above the water, because my head collided with asphalt,' I say.

Jusuf said, 'Fuck it, I'm really sorry that happened to you. And I believe you love him. You can only fall like that when you're young. It's normal.'

Jusuf said: 'There was a girl, we were together for a few years, then it collapsed. The world collapsed, so why not the two of us. She went off with someone else later, had a baby. And when they asked her at the wedding how would it be if Srđan came, that's what I was called then, she said: "just don't let him come – I'd drop everything and go with him." But I didn't go, only all my life I've thought how I could go, that I'm on my wa, and yet I'm further away than ever. But do you know what the hitch is? If we'd stayed together I wouldn't love her so much, I think. That's probably why I didn't go. So I'd have someone to think good things of all my lousy life.'

'Well, the time has come for me to go, I've decided. Just need to meet him, see him and talk to him once more,' I say. 'Do you know about drawing-room revolutionaries, my dear?'

'There are such things,' says Jusuf.

'Well, I've been a drawing-room lover all my life. I've never done anything crazy. I wasn't like my characters,' I say.

'My father lost his mind several years before his death, we believe it was Alzheimer's, but picturesque. One day, Mother asked him: do you know who I am, Milan? And he said: I actually don't know, I don't know who you are, but I know that I love you,' I say.

Then he asked me, Jusuf: 'Are you frightened? Of that shit in your head?'

'No, I was at first, of course, very, but not any more. At times I even feel a sense of relief. This is like the end of the world, postponed, a wonderful time for me. When it comes, I shall be ready.'

He said: 'I get that, it's not that I don't get it, you'd like to get this story finished. But just think, what do you do if you are for him a person who, at any stage, if she remembers, could turn his whole life upside down, what if he leaves everything and follows you. There are such phenomena, people leave everything because of a fanny.'

'I'm not expecting that, sweetheart. But, it would be wonderful. Maybe for such people, excuse the expression, a fanny is everything,' I say.

'An idea without action is day-dreaming. Action without an idea is a nightmare. Is that right? A Japanese proverb. Well, now, straight up, just so you know: as far as I'm aware, Nightingale went to America, he needed a year to sort out that green card. He went to start a new life, found a job, he went off to that little black girl and her small daughter.'

He said that just like that, in passing, as he might have said it was getting cold, autumn's coming or I'll go and light up, you come in a while. I was left alone in the Red School. *After wars comes joy and an eruption of sexual freedom,* was written above a dissolute drawing on the wall. One I'd seen on some Norwegian or Swedish portal. Above another, less depraved, it said: *If the effort of love is always lost, do I lose gladly?*

I sighed loudly and sat down with my back to the scene. But what was I expecting?!

LETTER FROM A PASSING CYCLIST

dear sir ve ovver evenin i call on my mate in simunović street i was ridin me bike from ve town to sirobuja district the evenin were bootiful it all smelled of tourism of creams and grilled fish cars hooted sloshed teens shouted to each ovver and i climing slow uphill enjoyin the souns of the street when fuckin ell my tyre bursts the front one wa's more don' do vis to me i finks wa' do i do now i won get vere till t'moro mornin and ven i decides to call on vat mate call him to let me sleep over cos he's got no car either a pawn like me an' to be brief vats vere i vent and got a real shock i never liked vat street cos you can't ride a bike normal-like on it unless you's a bmax bandit or 'as a mountain bike and ven only downhill, to go uphill you has to get off and clamber wiv yer bike on yer shoulder and my bike is a racer real one wiv fin tyres it don't leap down steps to cut it short vat's vere i 'eard you ven i fell asleep on vat friend's couch like a million times before and i couldn get vot ve fuck vos goin on i asked my mate vot ve fuck's goin on and e said can't you ere people are fuckin every goddam night around two or free it starts they're not normal no one can get a wink you wouldn bleive it brill I say like an idiot and wake up in a flash i tell im i've not talked like vis since ten years ago wiv my firs luv in me at primary school in ve las' year she was so neat you couldn' look at her an she wos clever and funny and ve were like togevver and in ve firs year of secondry she wos even lovelier but ven becos of her as she wos shamed by er mates ve vere only friends cos we wos too young for intimate relations and i wos crazy wiv jealousy cos i really loved her

on my life more van my life i would av done anyfing for her and
ven at the end of ve first year she moved away somewhere abroad
she went cos of the war everyone moved somewhere out of split or
belgrade or zagreb and er dad got to be some bigwig in the county
and quickasaflash vere goes ve girl to school in italy art school she
wasn't great shakes as a student and i was left in the shit and went
looking for er in every woman ten years ago i was a couple of streets
down by ve sea ridin my bike and run into some woman i nearly
said wot you doin not lookin where you goin when she says ello
you why you're joe but you don' remember who i am and who are
you i ask and she says she's the one and i can't believe it it's not true
she's totally changed not vat she's got fat or much older but she as
grown into an ugly woman and she ad been i told you a real little
merry beauty i wos beside meself nuffin worse could ave appened
was this that love of my life how is it possible we sat down and ad a
few drinks i was shakin from one shock after another it wos er by her
voice an her gestures but far far uglier and sadder the more i drank
the more her gestures stood out and her voice and her ugliness and
some emptiness in er talk fell into the background and we recalled
memories we went to mine to light up some grass an when finally
we grabbed each other it wasn't possible to stop I screwed the idea
vat she wos my old love whose picture i had built up from childhood
all these years we adn't seen each ovver up down missionary from
behind i was totally on fire wiv sex like on viagra bruvver the girl
didn't know wot ad come over me all the accumulated tension in
connection wiv her came back to me but it very soon left me and
instead came sorrow cos the one i had so long ago fallen in love wiv
wos no longer not only in appearance but altogevver the girl was a
bit miffed cos she jus couldn't get wot woz appening first we screw
like romeo and juliet and then i could no longer bear to see her i
was desperate vat i wos so superficial but in fact i wosn't cos from

the shock i fell into a deep depression from which i ave not got over even today i tried being wiv ovver women and wiv two men i spent myself which is not really for public knowledge and vere vos good sex and attraction but no real love vere vos a ole in the middle of me as vo vey ad pulled out me lungs i can't relax any more comin' wosn't nuffin from stress and insomnia as before i gave meself up to drugs and drink more van ever but not too much jus' enuff not to crack up vat's worse van when someone close dies cos my ideal ad died and wos now walking about like a zombie says my mate from šimunović street wen i told im all vis vat e ad a similar fing wiv is former wife but she didn't become a zombie but a diva which means vat in relation to im it wos the same as er being dead just vat she was now livin in some paradise where ovvers use er and you read about it in the papers god grant none of vis appens to you vat's wot i wanted to say good luck folks and use condoms wisely and that…

The Red School is a place of love, murder and death. It's an abandoned building in the middle of nowhere that closed at the beginning of the 1970s when there were no longer enough children in Tulumbe and the surrounding hamlets. It was built on a road that leads nowhere in peacetime, and along which in wartime every army passes, for the borders are right here, over every hill. In war, an army passes, one displaces, the next burns, a third, triumphant, slaughters. Legend has it that the white walls of the former school could not be cleansed of the blood of the young just-married husband and wife, teachers in this same school in which they were killed in the Second World War. The bloody stains penetrated the walls until someone hit on the idea of painting the school red, so the legend goes. In any case, Helanka's father and other relatives attended the school, and then it moved from this building to a village several kilometres away, but here, until the last war, it was possible to find the old registers with pupils' marks. (Terribly bad marks, laughed Helanka. Not everyone was a star pupil in those days.) Later, later, the building was a slaughterhouse (that's the logical reason why it was repainted red), until the last war when, as the only surviving building in this region, it served as a shelter and shit-house for soldiers. Why didn't they crap in the fields? Fear of mines? Jusuf says that there shouldn't be any mines round here, but that is yet to be found out. Whether anyone was killed or tortured here will be found out too. Or maybe not.

Now the whole building is a bloody stain around which the whole of this empty landscape, all of nature, organises itself. And really, everything here is tranquilly idyllic, a pastoral setting until the school comes into one's line of sight and starts bleeding. Then the landscape is transformed into something ominous, into a place where one ought not to wait for nightfall. The heart of darkness in the garden of Eden.

The nations and nationalities here really got a kick out of killing teachers, I had noticed that. In every second village, where there had been a school, there is a memorial plaque. This was, statistically speaking, probably the category of civilian professions most frequently murdered in wars and the aftermath of wars in the Balkans. I imagine that they were shot in the head: the young teachers, a married couple, stood, clever and honest and still in love, as usual, in the classroom, by the lectern, beside the blackboard where there was a rubber and some pieces of chalk, he covered the crown of her head with his hands and she his face with her whole forearms.

A bird flew in through the broken window and fluttered about between the walls. I opened what was left of that window, then the other windows, let the light in.

He said he would come here, as soon as he could, and paint a mural for the murdered teachers and the bleeding school, Gale did (twenty years ago), but, Helanka said (twenty years ago): Not a chance. There's nothing here any more that art would not sully. (The graveyard, a hundred or so metres behind the school, visible from here too through the open window, has been transformed into a copse, crosses push into branches, while here and there tree roots have lifted gravestones, opening them up.)

The mural that Gale painted is called New Alexandria. It is painted in the huge space on the remaining supporting walls and over the remnants of the dividing ones. It looks wonderful in this bloody shell, the story of man: soul and flesh. It shows an imagined future for this region. (Utopia, why yes, utopia, what else, it's the duty of anyone living in a dystopia to create a utopia, my dear.)

The mural: the earth to the stars.

Abundance: high forests, corn, animals, houses, a school, sky-scrapers and mountains in touch with the clouds, people who leap and fly naturally through the rooms, people, mauve, green, gold, playing or working, in conversation, or an embrace, or at table, eating enormous fruit, having children, playing music and dancing, telephoning, and over them fly huge bees with great breasts from which honey and milk pour. Some merry fellows (or lasses) have big willies as well as tits. Gale had shown things they way they are. Life is sumptuous, only the news about it is bleak.

Here are the teachers, husband and wife, healthy and cheerful, scantily dressed. Happy and hale as at a lovely wedding.

Between the people and the animals are ropes up which they climb or cross from one side to the other, here are key words in various alphabets and languages: laughter, optimism, serenity, nobility, song, generosity, a little gift, an embrace, brilliant and abundant, life-giving, love, tickling, rapture, surprise, warmth… beneath the people and the plants grows a city of miraculous architecture, the soft physical forms of Gaudi and Niemeyer.

What kind of hand wrote such a palimpsest? It's not a child's. What kind of hand wrote such words in such a place? It wipes away death as though it were dust. Perhaps that's all that's possible, to reconquer the space. To bear life across death. What kind of eye painted this?

In one place, right in the corner, it says: The stallion's eye is not an asshole (The eye must be cared for? The eye looks, and doesn't crap? The eye is pure?)

On the north wall, exposed to a gleam of sun from outside, a luxuriant glimmering garden has burst into life with gigantic vegetation and produce among the wonderful skyscrapers. Two sunflowers on the roof have the twins' faces. The well has become a lake on the square with a lot of birds like fish and stars.

Over it flutters a slender water snake of verses:
Helanka's miraculous garden (and larder):
Sage for the throat
Camomile for the eye
Marshmallow for the nose
Wormwood for the stomach
Artichoke for the liver
Juniper for the teeth
Plantain for wounds
Vinegar for stings
Kefir for the pussy
Strawberry-tree berries for the cock
Cornel juice for sluggish intestines
Plums for motions
Bacon for cuts
Olive oil for a painful ear
Cabbage (leaf) for inflamed tits
Fennel for milk
Sage for stopping milk
Bread when a bone gets stuck in your throat
Chestnuts for veins
Honey for energy
Hierba Luisa for the heart
Hellebore for death
Lavender for the soul
Marijuana (leaf) for laughter
Marijuana (stalk) for oblivion
Rosemary for remembrance
Rosemary for remembrance
Rosemary for remembrance.

Then I heard footsteps and thought they were Jusuf's. (Just coming.) Through the Red School door came a tall woman with a dark cap, her face familiar. 'Who's parked illegally in the middle of the grass?' she asked. Then she burst out laughing gutturally, loudly, opening her arms wide towards me.

Helanka's face was an event. Her back was an event as well, broad and bony (twenty years earlier), and her whole bare body was not so much beautiful as exceptionally rare and otherworldly. On the boat or on the beach we had looked at her forever surprised all over again, looked at her and saw a unicorn and a golden blade. She had no eyebrows, she had no eyelashes, generally, she had always had that complete lack of fuzziness that has a medical name, but I would not call it a disorder, dear, because she was perfect (it's called complete Alopecia). And now forty, with some ten more kilos she was good-looking, wearier, more sensual and softer, with a sinful vertical line beside her lip, she had acquired something very feminine, earthly. When she was a little girl in the small town, her appearance bothered her (she had said that twenty years ago), but her interesting body richly rewarded that sacrifice when she grew up and set off into the wide world. Among the little zebras with pony-tails, with fragile legs and slender hooves, sexually anxious and therefore excessively brazen, when she appeared in Split, Helanka looked like a puma. That's how she moved, it's how she approached things and people, my dear. The glowing ball of her quick, feminine intelligence gleamed over our first conversations about serious matters, our first battles of wits. Had such a person been born in my town, we would have made her into a foreigner, she would have left at the first opportunity. As it was, she was already an outsider. One summer she came to visit her aunt, as she did every year, but by the autumn she no longer had anywhere to return to. A piece of good fortune in her misfortune was that the same chance events that had brought her aunt to this town, meant that Helanka happened to have been born in Split, so she acquired a Croatian passport. She said: 'I lied that I was a Croat, I don't give a shit, and I was born here. And they gave me that fucksport while my aunt who is married here and has lived here since nineteen sixty-eight, can't get a Croatian passport, because she was born in Drvar, Bosnia. She had to prove she was a Croat. They won't let her be one. You have to earn that honour. It's easier here to buy a degree and be a doctor of science than to acquire a Croatian passport,' she said.

She studied medicine, thanks to her refugee points, she said. And she was the worst student in the history of that faculty to graduate from it.

But, I say: in the street, she set things and people in motion. People who came from a certain distance were the ones who made things happen. Those who left went away to make things happen in some other place. (Twenty years ago and probably also today and always.) She was accepted, taken to people's hearts and for me my friendship with Helanka and Nightingale opened the doors of the town, back doors, hidden ones into an invisible parallel world which I had no idea existed. These were doors in the Palace and outside it on which one knocked when nothing else was working (the town was deserted, blacked-out, so doubly dark). Few came in, they brought the light of their eyes and cigarettes into the cellars, shelters, garages: a smile would blaze, a bare arm, radar, a dancing thigh. (Her thigh over his, his arm, his cruel ankle, soft and friendly on her snake-like neck.)

A ruptured friendship can jolt us to the core that is lost love, only without frenzy, without a safety valve. And I had abruptly lost them both. If you ask them, I had abandoned them. (Demagogues.) And maybe I did, maybe I was frightened of them and all that could have come our way from our life in that town in which we only had each other, and every winter was then long, dark and rainy.

In that circle everyone knew that Gale was a deserter. When we met he was sleeping under the counter of the little café where he had worked as a student, he couldn't go home. In the street you could hear all sorts of stuff about him.

That he had run away from his village to Split while still at school. (In fact he lived in a hostel for boarders.)

That his father had disinherited him when he signed up to study painting rather than carpentry. (His Dad was already deceased, and his Mum Josipa sold their vineyard to buy him the flat in Dinko Šimunović Street where she never set foot.)

That he was a womaniser. As far as I gathered, that was the male version of what is implied when one says 'loose woman'. He didn't cheat. 'In his case it was perhaps a case of serial monogamy,' I said. But he was offended if I harped on about that. Although at that time (twenty years ago) I didn't think like that, but I should probably have been grateful to those women, because I learned everything important that I know about love-making from Gale and he had been initiated into that skill by his former lovers, each in her own way. Just as my lovers in the years that were to come had something to thank Gale for: my assured and liberated body that was not ashamed of dancing, my naked body that was not ashamed of light or making love, which, in addition to giving, had learned also to take.

That he was a Croatian Ustasha. Our street said that too. Because he went to war against his Homeguard village of Mitrovići in Bosnia. We can't all starve ourselves so as not to fight, he said, not everyone has that context, my dear.

'If they come to the door of your flat (or village) and want to kill you and set fire to the flat, you a) run away and let everything go to hell, because it's not your war, and the flat is in fact your Gran's; b) you let the usurper set fire to you along with the flat, the building, the town and the village because you are opposed to violence;

c) you grab the first available weapon, a hunting rifle, pitchfork, or axe and try to drive the enemy into the shit,' said Gale. 'I think, all those responses are OK, but I know which is the most honest of them for me. (I reject violence. Except in self-defence.)'

That he was in fact a Serbian Chetnik. Because he was friends with Helanka, of whom it was said she was a Serb although she said she was Bosnian. Every Serb was a Chetnik, every Serb had a beard and carried a knife between his teeth, even old women and babies, that was common knowledge. But we loved everything that was terrible and disgusting in that moral little land of peasants, including those few remaining poor Serbs who kept justifying something to someone. Apart from Helanka who never justified herself even for things she maybe should have done.

Then – that he was a deserter. After a few months of war, his commander ordered him to return to his studies. Nevertheless, as soon as he had graduated, they summoned him back to war, again. This time to Bosnia. And he didn't respond. When the military police came to his door in Šimunović Street, he chose response a) and hid. He sent them a message: I reject all violence, except in self-defence! Naturally they thought: this guy's fucking us around.

'Something happened in his head in that war,' said his Mum Josipa. 'Something clicked.'

'He saw more clearly, quickly and better than us,' I say. 'In fact, we could see too, but unlike us he believed his eyes, while the rest of us closed them,' I say, 'and we squinted, we still squint today. He didn't get worked up to convince himself of the rightness of his actions, he didn't justify himself, if he did regret anything, he was just cleansing himself of the war, furiously and painfully, my dear.'

He wrote: *Patriotism is the last refuge of scoundrels.* (On walls.) *Love of country justifies the making of large numbers of murderers. Patriotism transforms a thinking being into a dedicated machine. Love of country is para-religious hogwash that produces inevitable damage if it is established as a criterion.*

It was almost impossible for something like that to happen in Split, but it did. In Split all sorts of things happen, the worst and the best. Love of country justifies the making of large numbers of murderers. Patriotism transforms a thinking being into a dedicated machine. Those were useful warnings, but they did not survive more than two or three days. They were painted over and on top of them people wrote the street hit ultimatum: *Abortion is murder.*

I liked what he said and did, because it seemed to me dangerous, but important. In that tedious war nothing happened (apart from the war) apart from Nightingale.

I told him: 'I know everything about you. People tell me you're a gangster, a robber, that you're a good-for-nothing, that you're a poker-player, a fucker, that you ran away from the war, that you came from some Serb backwater and that you're crude like all Serbs.'

He gave as good as he got. He said: 'Now I'll tell you what I've heard about you. You're a typical Split bitch, loud and la-di-dah, stuck-up, thick as a post and wicked as the devil.'

'Although you make great caramelized sugar.'

'Although you make great caramelized sugar.'

Then they caught him, beat him up. We think it was the Little Chief's gang, they just beat him round the head and kicked him about a bit. That's what he said. There wasn't any question of hiding in the café any more. Helanka brought him, black and blue, onto the boat with another lad from our group.

'He can't stay here. I'll be in trouble,' I say. 'What if, I don't know, the military police come?'

But Helanka said: 'Get her, she'll be in trouble. What kind of a little cunt are you.'

And she nearly burst into tears. So did I, for my own, unaltruistic reasons. 'But I am a little cunt,' I shouted, and they laughed.

'The boat's not exactly equipped,' I said. While I'm dying of fear. 'But let him stay till tomorrow. Only don't tell anyone,' I said. 'My mother will kill me,' (It's always useful to mention maternal authority.)

'Thanks,' said Gale, although he could barely talk, his tongue was bleeding, you couldn't make out what he was saying. 'I'll leave tomorrow.'

But he didn't leave. He lay on some old sheets and groaned in the night.

Nevertheless, my panic subsided. I enjoyed this concealment, as though it were stealing. I thought I was brave. I wasn't. But my fear and shame of Helanka and Gale, of their contempt, was greater than my fear of the military police.

At that time we definitely became mates, a trio. We played cards in the harbour, cooked and smoked on Woody Mary and waited, waited a long time for it all to die down. We waited in the cramped space of the boat's cabin that was warmed by making tea in salty pans, in a space full of the smell of bodies, oil, skin and inevitable brushing against each other. I can see him now in that pose, with a smoked cigarette he was chewing between his small even teeth, with his blond mane, wiry and firm, with his brown skin, squatting in my granddad's ancient Bermudas and repairing, forever repairing, oh sweetheart, always the same fault with the boat's engine. Or catching fish, or cooking tinned beans, or reading the paper, or when he decided to clean the entire boat with a piece of rag. Painstakingly, revelling in his devotion to each action.

'I'm a coward,' he told me. (We were sitting on the edge of the boat, eating watermelon, its juice dripping into the sea.) 'Luckily for me as a man, I'm only a coward appalled by war. Fuck off with your war, well away from me.' (He was a magnificent coward, truly refreshing in a land of heroes, if you ask me, my dear.)

One evening, he and I waited in vain for Helanka to turn up at the boat. Our conversation, without her, stuttered. For weeks before that I had laughed at his occasional switching on of his charm, childishly, but he didn't do it when we were alone. He's not remotely double-crossing me, I thought. I thought about him, my dear, I thought that I was on firm ground and I kept thinking that the poor man must surely have fallen in love with me. I kept thinking and thinking and fell in love with myself. But not remotely with him, my dear.

That evening he talked a lot (he was cheerful) and made tea, poured it into cups, always chipped and always a little salty from the sea. Then, he got serious, which he did not often do either. When he finally sat down, I suddenly stood up and sat down right on him, pressing against him with my whole body. 'I thought that you were fragile,' I told him then. 'But you're not.'

It was an experiment, my dear. I knew that on that kiss depended whether I would flee or stay (love or not, it always depends on a kiss). And I stayed. Before we realised what was happening, with entwined tongues swelling, with hearts swelling, with genitals swelling, we were unexpectedly naked and clambering all over one another, fighting for air. No one moved to close up the boat and the wind kept flapping the hatch-cover and disclosing a piece of the night. Or maybe it was raining and drumming on the prow. Or else it was calm and the plankton was crackling. Then I no longer heard or saw anything other than him, bending over me and begging: 'Look into my eyes.' I had slept with others, but I had never looked anyone in the eyes while screwing, apart from Nightingale.

'The girl's humped you, you idiot,' said Helanka the next day as soon as she set eyes on us. We peered out from down there in the cabin, sinful and tousled. 'You disappoint me,' she said, sticking out her tongue, 'you'd have been better off with me.'

That was the summer when the Czech tourists returned. Things no longer looked so bad even for deserters. Gale walked barefoot over the beaches, drawing portraits of tourists for a bit of cash, shouting happily: 'The Czech Republic on sea!'

I sold Italian ice-cream. *Zuppa inglese* was my favourite. When we had earned a bit we'd go crazy, having fun as long as the money lasted. So, the Czech Republic was back on the sea, *Zuppa inglese*, brown arms, bare feet and salt in our hair, our eternal summer, our true homeland.

Three months later we married. We were so young: Nightingale and Clementine. Everyone was amazed, Ma (oh, Ma) went berserk. I was eighteen, and he was twenty-three (twenty years ago, roughly twenty years). Three years later we parted.

I went off to Zagreb, saying I'd be back, he said he'd come and, although that's what we wanted, it turned out we were both lying.

I went off to Zagreb, saying I'd come back, that my interest in soaps wouldn't last a lifetime, that I was going just to earn some money, but I was lying, things opened up and I went from one thing to another, they were attractive, but bad, they were glamorous and hollow and fun. I was going somewhere, moving forwards and forwards was ever further away from Dinko Šimunović Street, from the marina and the boat and our story in which we had collected enough small coins for a pizza or a coffee. The new town sucked me into its enchanting spaces, into unexplored places (how soon all that would bore me). Everyone liked me, all clothes suited me. He said he'd come, but he no longer cared so much about me. Once he appeared at a party in those camouflage pants of his, a little lost, subdued and cynical. And it seemed to me that I didn't care so much about him either. I was even ashamed, and maybe he was ashamed of me. When we were alone, things were as they'd always been, but among people – all those people came between us.

He began regularly drawing cartoons for newspapers, for a while he had a job at the Art School ('I've got a job, come back now, better you come to me, I can't, no') and although that's not what we wanted it turned out that we were lying, my dear. 'And who are we to have gone on being happy? Who can bear that,' he said (that he was leaving me). 'You're right, better part as friends.' (If the effort of love is always lost, do I lose gladly? But what did I know about that in those days, that the same thing was not waiting for me every Saturday and that no one else would ever hold me and look me in the eyes like that. That in truth no one else would ever really converse with me.)

I went to bed and slept for three days. Maybe I would have slept forever, but on the third afternoon Kalemengo came and brought me soup and grilled some meat. We ate off the ironing board, because I had still not bought a table. Between two mouthfuls he said some scientist maintained quite seriously that we could live to 150 if we just gave up love-making. We went on chewing in silence for a few moments. Then Kalemengo added: 'What do you think – does that mean that nuns and priests do fuck after all?' And: 'You know, I have an unrealisable desire to produce a soap that takes place in a monastery … It would be relatively chaste, I promise.'

It was fairly entertaining in my tragic circumstances.

That's how it was at the time when Gale left me. Helanka said: 'He just let you go. You were the one who left us. Now you have grown up.'

Demagogue.

I looked for her in Split for several weeks after that. Nor was Gale in Šimunović Street: when I unlocked the door of the flat my remaining things were waiting for me in the hall, tidily packed into a few boxes. I set off to the harbour, Gale was usually there mending the boat, but the Woody Mary wasn't there either. After a whole year on dry land, our boat had finally sailed again, without me. (They sailed away. They sailed away without me. They sailed away. Without me.)

I didn't get in touch with her for a long time, and then several years later I picked up the phone. We didn't mention Gale. 'How're things there?' I asked when we spoke that first and last time. She had finished her degree after quite a long time. ('Congratulations'.) She said: 'Things are good if you're in the hospitality trade, the tourists have come back, hordes of them, all kinds. And they don't leave. I think it's time for me to move away. Or kill myself. Or get married. I'll reflect on it.'

But I no longer had the will to listen to her reflections. Should we just chat? She was important to me forever, but she belonged to the past.

Now she was somehow larger, Helanka. And she didn't look like a capricious hot-headed nymph, more like a sorceress.

Behind Helanka her daughter Arrow shot into the Red School.

Behind Arrow came her sister Billy Goat.

Tea and Meri. Who knew whether they were Danny-Boy's children? That crossed my mind.

'Everyone follows his star.' (Jusuf had disappeared some time before, Jusuf with no star.)

'That was yesterday. Today I am already on my way to another place.'

Helanka stood between her daughters who fell on her with embraces, softer than I remembered her. I recalled the way my mother used to ask: 'What are you going to write about, my daughter? No one who doesn't have children knows anything about life. Anyone without children has only himself to worry about.' (And

I wanted to throttle her, full of hatred for her limitations, poor Ma, but maybe she was right.) When the girls finally fell away from Helanka, we were left alone.

Helanka said: 'I came at once, as soon as they told me. They said you had issues with your head? But you look fine to me.'

She looked concerned. We gazed at each other and for some time could not move our eyes away. Where to start and what should we talk about now, apart from illness? Best to talk about the weather, dear. About the children! 'Your children are wonderful.' Yes, her daughters are the love of her life, her joy and fear. She lives for them. Although, there were times when it was unbearable, no one prepares you for small children, that endless feeding and accompanying activities.

'Women are always blackmailed by their children – there's no way out of it!' she said.

'Apart from in my case,' I say.

'Yes,' she says vaguely, 'yes.'

But they soon won't be children any longer. And they will abandon her.

'Better to have your heart broken by children than men,' she said.

'And the mountain garden? It's beautiful and useful. It has everything. And all healing.'

She is more useful here than when she was dressing varicose legs in the dispensary.

'Permaculture, self-sufficiency, return to nature, altered blood count, local cooking,' she says.

Children, plants and animals, that's what she's surrounded herself with. She needs tender and wild creatures, but husbands – she said that in the plural, now, at this time of my life – only for physical activities. She laughed again, and so did I, although I may not have found it all that funny. (That was yesterday, today I'm already on the road to a different place.) I loved her, not like before, but forever. I hope she knows that.

She said: 'Come, and take a look. Someone's waiting for you outside.' (Nightingale?! That's not possible. Bert? Maybe my brother?)

I peered through the door (through the opening in the house without a door) and in the Mazda in the passenger's seat saw my destiny – Kalemengo. Even older than before. (He's 150 years old, a white hat and wonderful silk suit.)

He was smoking a fat cigar. Sheep were bleating round the car.

He called out: 'So, tell us, who is the man of your life?'

Did I already say that there were sheep bleating round the car? There must have been seventy white and the occasional black one from one of the neighbouring villages. Unbelievable. They were guarded by a large shaggy dog. The sun had risen and filled the air with green and gold insects.

Kalemengo said: 'How are you, Piccola? For God's sake!'

I sat down beside him, kissed his dry, fragrant cheek. Here I somehow cracked up and let a tear, maybe two, maybe even ten, fall. He patted me on the shoulder. I closed my eyes, pressed the brake, turned the key and started the Mazda.

I said: 'It looks as though I'm better than I thought.'

LETTER FROM AN UNBORN POET

One day they'll ask you, my dear mother, whether I'm ill. 'Forgive me, is there something wrong with your little girl?' That will be the first criticism of my poems. Why would a child write if it was well? Why, there are so many things to be consumed, to be run around. Those are all healthy things for the young. But you'll tell them, Ma, because you'll love me even when you don't understand me, that I write and read in the fresh air as well and that looking at words develops my sharpness of vision, that I see through my skin, that from writing my fingers are already huge for my age and that in fact I don't spend very much time writing, but rather observing, which often hinders your conversation with me. Our acquaintances, when we aren't there to hear them, will conclude among themselves: How can such a small being produce a new reality, a new language, where is her raw material, her tools – it's too much, the child will go mad before she's twenty or so. But of course I won't. I shall grow firmly into everything I touch, it will be hard to demolish me if not because of love.

I shall take every object and turn it round a hundred and eighty-five times, sniff it and lick it. For my profession it's important to know the taste of wood, the smell of a nail, the qualities of material, the foundations, if you want to build a text. I shall run constantly up and down the same street until I can do it with my eyes closed, on one foot, even in fifty years' time. Depending on its components, I shall take every word apart into grains of gunpowder, neutrons or hairs and dust, and I'll shift every mouthful about with my tongue until savoury becomes sweet, and sometimes the other way round. As a poet, I must first be a sportswoman, a scientist, a double agent, if not, let's say a farmer. But still, time will always pass slowly for me, I'll live season by season, so that things manage to ripen. I shall not be cleverer or more sensitive, or braver than others, just more detailed. Out of that detailed knowledge of everything I come across in this world, I shall make a few thousand poems, of which a hundred or so will be frequently repeated by some people in their heads, as though they were singing.

One day they'll ask you, my dear father: 'Why does your child write terrible and peculiar things?' But you, my father, because you love me and understand me better than you thought you would know, will tell them that this is a matter of stylistic skill: practising figures of freedom. That practice either alarms or people don't need it. People constantly sing about freedom, but at the same time with all their limbs, including their tongue, they stay on the border. Well that's human, you have to understand that. You'll carry me when I get tired and, just like that, you will buy me books, you'll play tennis with me and I'll tell you when I get my first period. Our relationship will be decisive for my profession. Your early death will be decisive for my success. In a writerly sense, it will make me ancient and shameless. Beside mine, other people's words will often seem fearful and bloodless, or like those children's games in a safe room. Everything delicate and fragile that I shall create will come from muscles full of strength. For everything else, I shall learn to use books and from them I shall tirelessly cut out and steal a whole life.

You don't yet know that I'm with you, that we're here together, while you make love: my trusting parents, my parents full of trust, I'm coming to meet you and, at some stage, you will be the signature beneath each of my words.

Write this on the box, and we'll put everything away in it until it's needed... Okay? What if I don't even know how to read? Why I've got you to read for me, my dear. Write! I've recorded this for you. I began to record it in the month of September 2014. Your name is Clementine. The events, people, thoughts mentioned here were yours. I hope they will help you to feel who you are. It's about something that was particularly important to you. The letters read here were written by Nightingale, your first husband.

I've still got so much more to say, the question is will I have time?

There, when I've done that I can go further away. I can go to America.

PART TWO

Detroit

Opportunity is rare, where it occurs it should be accepted.
Diary of a Seducer, SØREN AABYE KIERKEGAARD

Peščenica district, Zagreb, Dinko Šimunović Street, March 2016.

A man appears on the screen, sitting in a black jacket under a tree in front of his building, which is in Detroit, a woman's voice says:

'There is a black dog with a wet coat sleeping across his shoes, and then the scene changes and that same man, only without the jacket, in a shirt and jumper, is sitting in a room in which every wall is a different colour and the two alternate: his picture outside and his picture in the room with the painted walls on a wooden chair, he is a middle-aged man, more blond than brown-haired and he speaks calmly, but in a lively way, he is asked something about inheritance, the reporter asks and the man talks about his forebears and his childhood and often gesticulates, and his hands are bigger than his face when he talks about his great-grandfather who was the first in the man's family, as far as it is known, to have written a graffito, and his great-grandfather had been very tall and he had written something on the wall on the way out of the town when he left Split, angry and disappointed, to go into the hills, to the Zagora district, where he founded his village, and that inscription stayed there for a long time, because it was written high up and it was clearly visible, because there were not many walls, and especially not walls with inscriptions in that part of the town, proclaiming *Split, I shit on your streets and on whoever returns to you*, as the man's great-grandfather had written, a merchant with creditors breathing down his neck because of his debts, "He had sold all he had left, did not pay off his debts, but took his money and never returned to Split nor did he allow anyone to mention the town to him," stated the man in Detroit with the big hands, adding that for the first year his great-grandfather had lived like a hermit, with animals, and then he set up a commune, some time before socialism and he employed people and people came to live with him, including women, peasant women who wore wide dark skirts and all that could be glimpsed of their figure were just their bare lower legs, which inflamed the men, and of course the men's excitement excited some women, and under a fig tree his great-grandfather gave a woman with strong ankles a son who was the grandfather on his father's side. The man, an artist from Detroit, on the screen, said that grandfather became famous in the region for his distinctive 'Hey!' mountain country songs, of which the man from Detroit sang a few seriously, frowning slightly:

Hey, my little one, machine-guns are crashing,
I'll come to you – never mind the shells smashing!
Hey, my little one, they're pounding your papa dear –
using hot tongs to curl his hair!
I've shaved and trimmed my own beard,
at the hearth where maize gruel's prepared!
Little one, turn your shutters back,
as climbing in I scraped my back!
My little one wants to pull,
she's stuffed her tiny bra with wool!
My little one, when you go to the hill,
tie your panties tight with twill!
Hey, wherever there's a clearing soft and green,
my shoulders' imprint may be seen!
Hey, give it to me, little one, if you want to be with me,
if you don't, don't fuck with me!

Grandad-the-singer had a wife who did not appreciate folk traditions, "She did not appreciate 'Hey!' mountain songs, jigs, ditties or traditional embroidery," said the man in Detroit. Apparently, she would sometimes beat her husband up, which was a terrible disgrace and he was laughed at behind his back, sometimes teased openly and as a result he was unhappy and drank a lot, while that woman who beat her husband hated everyone, and loved only one man, her son, the father of the man on the screen who was now saying that his father had no patience with art, he had more time for engines and hoes, although he was a university graduate, he taught technology in the district school, but on the other hand his wife, the mother of the guy from Detroit, embroidered a lot of scarves, tablecloths and tapestries of which the best known is the one showing the Mona Lisa and then they showed several artworks of the Mona Lisa drawn round about on walls using a special technique that resembled his mother's tapestry, and they also showed his mother in her village, a short-haired older woman, with a wonderful brown scarf with orange marigolds round her neck sitting on a bed under the Mona Lisa in a child's room, and on the table beside her there was a mouth-organ and to begin with she shed a few tears and wiped them away with her plump hands, but she did not speak nicely about her son the artist – it seems she was quite angry with him, because he had forgotten her, and at that he simply said: "That was my bedroom," and passed his hand through his hair that was greyer than blond or brown, and mentioned that he had been awarded a prize for his art work, a very significant one, international, and in connection with that he added: "There, you see, if you take my art away from me, I'm a real Croat, a Balkan man, that's how it is, I even fought in the war which is yet more proof that I'm a stereotype and where I come from my colleagues regard people like me as boring, peasants, and I don't blame them, it's true," that's what he says, he's serious, sitting in his jacket, but his eyes are laughing.

He says that when he was fourteen he moved to Split, to a hostel for school pupils, and in the background we see the town of Split, the sea glistening, some old walls and columns, monumental – that's Diocletian's Palace, clock towers, the sky, then skyscrapers, tall buildings, that's a district of Split, Trstenik, and Dinko Šimunović Street, where he once lived. Then the man said that this street was designed for people who moved to Split from inland – these were great internal migrations – but later many of them returned to those villages, hamlets, small half-dead towns. Dinko Šimunović himself, after whom the street is named, came to Split from the hinterland.

"They had to live somewhere, they had come to work here, there were jobs. I asked the architect who designed Dinko Šimunović Street about it. The architect told me that many people had accused him of having built dormitories in which no one dreamed, that he had made cold communities. That stung him, because he had wanted to make a real street, urban, with flats that would be homes, a street in which people would have to bump into each other. He said, the architect, that the district had been populated by empty people, they had come to the town, but had left everything they loved behind in their villages. A man without his loves is empty. He just waits to get his job done and escape for the weekend back to his home, to his loves, which are already former. That's why the architect, a sensitive and intelligent man, had designed a street in which people had to say good morning to each other, in which they could not pass each other in silence, a Mediterranean street of encounters, in which people really lived. But it was only partially successful, indeed it succeeded to quite a small extent. However, that dear, wise architect had forgotten one thing. In those buildings, in that street children grew up and it became their street for their whole lives. In it, whether they liked the street or not, all their future loves and convictions were conceived. Those buildings, those streets were the frame for the story of their lives. They went out into the street to meet and linger, they would sing about it or tell stories about it, just as I myself do, only all in different, our own, ways."

Dinko Šimunović Street in Detroit was now on the screen, that's what they call it and that's the street where my man lives and works and sits on a bench or an ordinary chair, wooden, in a flat with different coloured walls, but this street doesn't resemble its namesake in Split from a little while before, because the buildings are made of brick, and the houses with real gardens or courtyards had once been fine, expensive houses for one or several families, but now the district was deserted, the town was run down, there was no industry, there were no workers and the screen now showed images of gaping buildings and desolation and the last snow of the year was falling, as sleet. *How would we ever get over losing our minds? You see, we almost lost Detroit that time* – the song was playing in the background.

"I'll tell you how it all began. But, mind, it's quite a melancholy tale, even pathetic. You've been warned. I lived in a town that didn't want me, in a street that didn't like me, loving for at least half my life a woman who didn't stay with me all that long. What is more, I fought for foolish reasons for an absurd state, a quasi-state dominated by reactionaries, criminals and vergers, a state I profoundly despise (I don't enjoy talking about this). Although my parents loved me in their way, we didn't understand each other. I despised them and was afraid of them, and there were days when I would have been capable of killing them. I told them they were idiots, and then they wept. The art to which I dedicated my life was not able to support me, I did various other jobs, I spent most of my time on them, but that's OK. You see, when it's presented like this, my life is wretched, my most important loves weren't really reciprocated, but I can't say I was unhappy, at least not most of the time. I was never an embittered savage. Most of the time I was well, not exactly ecstatic, but tranquil and joyful. Because here are the facts: I had a town I loved, lived in a street I loved, I loved my wife and my parents, I loved my vocation, I even loved the country where I lived – at least the part of it I knew – except when I hated it. Home is where you are accepted, not where you were born or where you live. So, where is my home? Nevertheless, everything I have listed, I had and loved. I was not unhappy."

My man walks through the city through empty corridors and the halls of factories and through the railway stations of Detroit as though he was walking through the exhausted, sick, grey, but wonderful towns of Eastern Europe, he says, but it's sleeting, it starts to rain and the old snow has melted and the grey city is full of muddy puddles and the remains of snow and the man shivers, he is not slender or elegant, but he looks well-proportioned and sturdy, all of a piece, he does not look as though his limbs or his head are going to fall off, and he stops in front of a large building in which there was once a bank, but it is now a ruin with broken glass into which the wind has blown rubbish.

"In my country, as in most countries of the world, banks rob people. I once wrote a poem about how banks like that should be blown up – I sometimes write poems, I don't blow banks up. Someone once really did blow a bank sky high and left the title and some lines of that poem of mine on the wall. Wrote it on the wall. It took them nearly a year to find me. People don't read a lot of poetry." He laughs and covers his eyes with the tips of his fingers, but you can see his lips are moving.

"Life is mostly trivial, vulgar. They found me through a blog, with my name on it. I don't like being accused because of a joke or a poem. The people who denounced me were people I had lived with most of my life, I was separated from them by just a few metres of air and isolation. There are places in the world where people are killed because of poems, quite legally. My place is not like that, but you have different kinds of death sentences and dying, some kill you slowly. There was a man in the bank, a porter, they hadn't expected him to be there. He was my neighbour and he lost a leg. When we met on the street, he swore at me and turned his head away. The police let me go quickly, but I was guilty, my neighbour without a leg had to have someone to blame. Later they found the people who really were guilty, kids, activists, to whom a terrible misfortune had occurred – if you mess around with weapons someone innocent always suffers – but for my street I was still the guilty one. And so, I felt I had to leave."

"I have a daughter whom I hadn't met, but I love her and want to care for her. She lives in a small town near Chicago, which isn't very far from here. I looked for a place I could go to and I found Detroit, the city of Sixto Rodriguez and Eminem and other poets, Gil Scott-Heron…"

On the screen the mayor appeared, wearing a silk scarf, and a jacket, with a red face, saying that several years earlier, in his first mandate, he had invited artists to liven up the stweets, he put buildings at their disposal, a whole distwict and told them he wanted them to enwich the city, and so pwotect Detwoit fwom the gangs living in squats, and the artists attwacted touwists, the touwists attwacted shop-keepers, cafés, little westauwants, they attwacted a small industwy of souvenirs, the small industwy of souvenirs attwacted new artists, they founded a distwict theatre and people came to see the deserted city and the city was no longer deserted, and my man added: "I'm interested in these places without people, especially since I've been a person without a place, since the world became a sad place through which people roam seeking a home. Looking for empty places for empty people, an opportunity to start all over again.

"Such places appeal to me. Vacancy, which until recently or some time long ago, pulsed with life. Those vacant places are eloquent about life. Chernobyl has the loveliest dreams about life as it used to be, about chlorophyll, about good genes. Damask beneath the ash and corpses conceals a flower. If only Eros survives, minimal joy and defeated good will again win through. When Vesuvius spilt over Pompeii, one wall survived and on it was a fresco of a phallus and the text hic habitat felicitas, happiness lives here. It could have been a vagina or a piece of fruit, that flower, something life-giving.

"Births, relationships, holidays, morning departures for work, bicycles, crowds in the street, kisses and waving, bazaars and markets, city lights – all ordinary things lost forever become magnificent in such places. Some would say that they bear witness to evil, fear and death or as in Detroit collapse, but that is a superficial way of looking, such places bear witness also to the life that once was and the all-present sorrow for it. What keeps us going is memory. Thanks to remembering how to dive into water, drink beer, go for a walk, swing on a swing or pick fruit, people have survived all kinds of things, they didn't go mad so they'd be able to do all that again or in order to remember it in someone's name, in honour of someone's life. Memory is the future. Memory is what we hope for. All the more so for the young whose lives are hard. All that is needed is just one moment of happiness for us to follow it all our lives like a beacon on the horizon. It would be honourable to be a misanthrope, but it makes no sense when we live in a dystopia. We need things that are funny and pointless, despised enthusiasm, in order to maintain the turning of the world. As soon as you stop, you begin to be threatened by harmless things: water, air, ants and worms. Unfortunately, I'm not a dreamer, I'm not one of those who get things moving, I need to be got moving. More than love of people, because there are all kinds of people, I am moved on by a taste for life. One should love and value life more, which is mostly difficult to do. However, without that we are all defeated."

The man had been drawn to the fact that the USA was where his daughter – from a liaison with an American he met one summer – lived, and he wanted to be closer to the child, says his colleague, a puma with an unusual cap, and she shows a picture of a little dark-skinned curly-haired girl with a plastic crown on her head, and then he heard that Detroit was looking for artist-inhabitants and he came, because the man was known for the fact that he went round empty places out of which people had moved by force of various circumstances and planned to found Dinko Šimunović streets in several deserted towns all over the world, wherever it was possible, and to fill them with replicas of souvenirs, replicas of real life, and this project is called Transfusion, people circulate through the world like blood, everything else is anti-nature, explained his colleague, a striking woman in an unusual cap, with no eyebrows, her legs crossed.

"When I left I didn't tell anyone, I didn't know exactly where I was going or what awaited me. I was running away from the man without a leg. I'm sorry that I didn't get in touch with my former wife. We looked for her, we wanted to invite her to the opening of the street in Detroit, but we were unable to find her. I think that she didn't want us to find her, but I hope that one day, on some outing, some sight-seeing trip, she will come across one of those Dinko Šimunović Street replicas of mine which are full of our lives. Look, I've even built a boat the same as the one in which we sailed, only it's made of cardboard. Where I come from there's a proverb – *settled accounts, long love* – but that doesn't have anything to do with love. If there were accounts in love, I would always be in debt … (to 'her' or to 'it'?)"

In the background is shut-down industrial machinery, a dead monster, harmless. It seems that snow is drizzling in Detroit again.

*

'What's this, a TV for just one person?'

'Is she watching that documentary again?'

'Her programme, again, Meri. And every day, the same one. She gets dolled up, puts on lipstick and watches it. Loud enough for the whole building to hear it.'

'Listen, Tea, I asked her why it's such a big deal and she said that man was her husband.'

'Imagine, she chose that loser, who just whines the whole time, while she doesn't even greet Robert, her real husband, when he comes. Nor her children. She says she doesn't have children. But I'd bet she does, she just hides them.'

'So does she really have some connection with that guy on TV?'

'Oh come on, what's with you, the man's never heard of her, she saw him when that programme was on and recorded it, and now she's rubbing our noses in it. Is that her husband? The director Kalemengo confirmed he was. Just as when she said she used to write soaps. Or that her younger brother was a doctor.'

'You mean a physiotherapist.'

'No, Jusuf is a physiotherapist, no, the young doctor, who visits us, I mean. I know what I'm talking about. And she got hit in the head, that's why she doesn't remember things. She's unhinged. She says she's forty, but she's more than sixty, she can try to cover it up, but the arms and neck say it all. She's not that much younger than us.'

'And that recording, where she recorded her voice: about herself and him so as not to forget.'

'Yeah, and that's a big enigma: who did she pinch all that from? Is that her voice on the recording? I haven't heard it. The director doesn't know. And anyway, what if it is, she probably made it all up on purpose. People will do anything to get attention.'

'She was a writer, that's what she says, and now she can't write so she records. She said she'd like to dictate a letter to me, because she can't see properly. I don't know, Tea. Maybe she has a lover?'

'A lover, my arse. She should be told she's out of line, complaining again. I'm against protection in our institution. The television in the day room is for all of us, because it's the biggest, the only one that works, and it's not hers. Whenever I come in, she's watching it. Let her go to her room.'

'There's no DVD in the room.'

'So, let them set up a computer for her.'

'But maybe she has a lover boy. Or girl, I know those women, that's the type, it's their life's calling. I don't mind that.'

'What d'you mean a lover? She hasn't, how'd she get that, the guy's in America. She's imagining it.'

'Imagining, not imagining, so what if she believes it. All that matters is believing.'

Detroit. Michigan. Dinko Šimunović Street, March 2016.

'There's a letter for you.'

'Thanks, Helanka! Leave it on the table, I'll look at it later, I have to take Pironi for a walk.'

'It's that unknown woman from Yugoslavia again. Why does she write to you in English?'

'She probably heard me speaking English on the documentary. And I have to tell you that there hasn't been a Yugoslavia for twenty or thirty years. But OK, you're right.'

'Bosnia, Czechoslovakia … I can't get my head round it all, my dear. You don't pay me for that. Aren't you interested in what she says?'

'I'm not sure this person can write, maybe she dictates to someone. The last time she sent me several cassettes as well. It's interesting.'

'I must confess I'm a bit proud of my role. You presumably don't want us to try and get a ban? Do you want to contact her?'

'No, I don't think that's necessary, although I would like to meet her.'

'If you ask me, that wouldn't be a good idea.'

'Probably not, unfortunately. Besides, I've checked, there's no proper name or address. There's no one with that name in Croatia.'

'Oh yes, Croatia's where you're from …'

'I've thought about it and this is what I think: she's built an entire emotional and erotic life on the basis of a few things she's happened to hear on a TV programme and who knows where else.'

'Like an Excel spread sheet?'

'Confabulation. I think that's what it's about.'

'Whatever. But, you know, it's a romance, man. Emotions can't be made up.'

'I wouldn't bet they can't be! Art is based on learned, un-lived through emotions, on observations. Romantic ideals, collected from books, films and poems demand of us that we idealise good sex. They push us to fantasise connecting ourselves to someone with whom we share only multiple orgasms or not even that, just fantasies about it. And so on in a circle.'

'You mean, love doesn't exist?'

'Love exists, of course, but it's not accessible. That's what this lover-girl of ours says too. Unhappy people feel happiness, think of gypsy celebrations, film stars kill themselves en masse, who is most afraid of the sea – experienced mariners, arrogance is a characteristic of the insecure, envy comes where it would be normal and decent to expect respect or even admiration, cynics are often those who care too much, the good suffer from their conscience, the evil swear by their good intentions ... Come on, enough about the logic of emotions. But, given that no one up to now has loved me even remotely like this woman, why shouldn't I enjoy it a bit.'

'Yes, shame her fellow isn't you at all, you monster.'

'It doesn't matter that I'm not the one, the main thing is she loves me. Isn't that always the case? Almost always. Often.'

'You go, and I'll read the letter, I can't wait. Take that animal out and buy me a bun on the way home. Please.'

'Are you reading it? Shall I take a look after all?'

'Here, it seems she's leaving you. I'm sorry, that's what she says.'

'What a pity. I'll miss her. Mad women know how to love.'

'At least you have some memories.'

CLEMENTINE'S LETTER TO NIGHTINGALE

Darling,

it's so hard for me to talk to you, after so many years of silence and knowing in advance that you won't hear me. To talk, in fact, to myself, but in order to tell the truth (we are most assiduous in lying to ourselves). Leaving you was the hardest thing I ever did in my life. When we met, we were very young, we consisted only of tense hearts out of which came tense limbs. We depended on one another like a pair of skaters on the ice, for a while. It was a samba, a flaming summer dance, on the tips of our skate blades. Before you, I was a child, almost nothing, an intimation, a being with no edges, a little denser than air. The child that I was could have become anything. Beside you, I began to be someone. The way I am, you would say ruthless, as I freed myself from you, I could not stay. You wouldn't like what I've become in the meantime. I had to peer behind hundreds of curtains, into several thousand eyes, between dozens of pairs of legs, into a certain number of wine glasses, as well, and in the end into a well, where I left my sight, my memory.

Today too statistics say: young people are very conservative, young people are conformists, just like the old, they would fuck without going in, they would steal if only they weren't seen, they wouldn't kill except in war. But not us (this former truth flatters me), we were children of a different class, street children, we loved those who were choosing their desired directions outside the trend – better towns, better love, better happiness, better something. Today I believe that in fact these endless directions chose people, because I too became like that, passionately directed, made to seek; I would never go back, you knew that and it took us in opposite directions. We were fragile upright statues who devoured each other with their eyes and fed on words, but with empty pockets, composed of pure expectation, and we did not want to die, but death was flourishing around us – it was not clever to have expectations. I was seventeen, then twenty and I wanted to live: that was my resistance to the monstrous carers of humanity, the amateur-generals, militants who sprang up everywhere, making demands, everyone made demands, they strung up around the world a wire cage of demands and hatred and then they invited me, us, to take responsibility for it. I shat on their creation of reality, just as now, my flag was always transparent and fluttery. My flag was sometimes also my skirt. I wanted my private Odyssey, I couldn't wait for our un-worked-through youth to become a humiliated and decrepit youth, marking time forgotten in front of a closed cinema; old young men and girls with the habits and clothing of adolescents always saddened me. The apex of life ought not to be our school days, at just the outset, before you are even a person. The thought of getting stuck in such a potential person, in such an un-prodigal being for my whole life, that frightened me just as much as the only other available possibility offered free by life – that you should fill in a form in your twenties, make a contract with your own destiny: home, job, marriage, children or a dog, engagement in social networks, a grave secured in good time. Any other kind of life is dearly paid for and, when I left you, I paid for it with my bleeding heart. But I had everything else. Arms, legs, head, eyes, lungs, that thing.

I remember you as a young soldier, a homeless deserter, before love, and afterwards as a young sea god with a crown of aluminium foil declaiming a poem on our kitchen table or standing tall against the mast on top of the boat's cabin, and coming towards me, always naked, always with a clean body and erect member: there is something touching and tender in that image, something that wants to wrap around me like my legs, as it always wanted. But before we undressed, you would envelop me in words, straighten my cap in the street one winter (or maybe it was a hat for the spring-summer). Our conversations were never finished. You had everything: both style and courtesy. Softly coated inside and out, sensitive, with sharp edges. You were a good man, but wicked.

If over the years your anger with me has not been transformed into hatred or, even worse, indifference, but even then, perhaps you would like to know: whenever I was doing everyday, quite private things, taking care of my body, making sure that my face stayed smooth, and my hair shiny, that my teeth were healthy, and my muscles taut, whenever I tried new things, in food, in love, travelling, reading, listening to music, I fooled myself that I was collecting those experiences for you, building what could be built, endeavouring to preserve what was decaying. (I wanted to become someone who would amaze you when we next met, but I don't think you would have liked the result.) You were the hidden motive, the one for whom one got out of bed in the morning, the one from the past who was at the same time someone from the future. Something like hope, an attractive reward for the foreseeable future, that possibility that something could happen and at the same time fear of just that. All those years you were more (or less) a dream, which it is essential to dream as inaccessible, rather than a desire that had to be fulfilled. I didn't wait for you standing in the rain, but in drawing rooms, hotels, restaurants, on quays, squares, boulevards, avenues, in parks, sometimes alone, mostly in groups, enjoying myself. I learned to live without us, but in the foundations of my body there lingered the memory of you as trembling.

A lot of moving away from everything, that's what my journey consisted of, fleeing from anything that could have stopped me: you can make a mistake and pull in your wings just once, when you fall, you fall to the end, although mostly you don't even notice, because you fall infinitely gently and slowly (as though there won't be any blood). And now I'm here. I read your letters again and complete the sentimental biography of a spoiled, somewhat hysterical writer of romances and soaps who nevertheless still managed to be calculating too. But I could have written books in which everything looks lived through and real, rather than a life full of paper characters. Perhaps I could have gone on writing poetry, which you liked at that time. So did I? You can't be only partly in such a life, we know that. In this corner of the world such a me could not exist. You still have a chance that before you die you will be offered delicacies and that starlets will sit on your knee, maybe you'll be offered a TV show, but, if I had chosen an identical path, I would probably have ended up as a crazy old woman in poverty, fed by a tube. You knew that was the case and that's why you were the one who should have come to me, but you didn't, ever. (In any case you abandoned the people you loved, but we have that in common.) You mastered all the skills of your profession, you became a ruler over words and colours, your talent remained on the ramparts of important things, but *I loved you more*.

But again, despite all my efforts at evasion, I did not avoid my destiny, like in those social games in which every time, no matter what the dice throw up, you are led inexorably to the same destination. In the meantime, by way of consolation, I played in my own way: with a lot of sixes and some lost lives, excitingly enough. Now it is time for exhalation, to let out everything I have held back and float off down the current (this is so pleasant). You who collect souvenirs bring those small crackling skeletons to the little fire of your memory, while I shall be silenced by the first snow on the screen.

For just one year, maybe two, we were happy, and that derivative of an epiphany proved enduring, stirred up with the rest of time. This is sure proof that it was a matter of an infringement from several spheres of life, divine and godly pornography. That could explain why from the beginning to today love is forbidden. It's still forbidden. Can you say it isn't when that notorious fact is the source of all our life's stories?

Olja Savičević is one of the best Croatian contemporary authors and a representative of the so-called 'lost generation'. Politically and socially engaged, Olja's work has been included in a number of Croatian anthologies and international selections, including Dalkey Archive's Best European Fiction & McSweenys' Quarterly Concern. Her writing has been translated into over fifteen languages and her short story collection *To Make a Dog Laugh* won the prize for best young author in Croatia. Her collection of poems *Mamasafari and Other Things* was short-listed for the 'Kiklop Award for Best Collection of 2012', awarded annually by the Pula Book Fair. Her debut novel, *Farewell, Cowboy*, was widely reviewed in the UK and US and selected for WHSmith Travel 'Fresh Talent' 2018. *Singer in the Night* is her second novel, and is also set in her hometown of Spilt, Croatia.

Celia Hawkesworth worked for many years as Senior Lecturer in Serbian and Croatian at the School of Slavonic and East European Studies, University College, London. She has published numerous articles and several books on Bosnian/Croatian/Montenegrin/Serbian culture and literature, including the studies *Ivo Andrić: Bridge between East and West*, *Voices in the Shadows: Women and Verbal Art in Serbia and Bosnia* & *Zagreb: A Cultural and Literary History*. Among her many translations are two works by Dubravka Ugrešić; *The Museum of Unconditional Surrender*, which was short-listed for the Oxford Weidenfeld Prize for Literary Translation, and *The Culture of Lies*, winner of the Heldt Prize for Translation in 1999. Hawkesworth was again shortlisted for the Oxford Weidenfeld Prize in 2018, for her translation of *Belladonna* by Daša Drndić, which was also a runner-up for the new EBRD fiction in translation prize in 2018. Her translation of *Belladonna* also won the 2018 Warwick Prize for Women in Translation.

First published in 2019 by
Istros Books
London, United Kingdom www.istrosbooks.com

Copyright © Olja Savičević, 2019

First published as *Pjevač u noći* in 2016

The right of Olja Savičević, to be identified as the author of this work has been
asserted in accordance with the Copyright, Designs and Patents Act, 1988

Translation © Celia Hawkesworth, 2019

Typesetting: Davor Pukljak, www.frontispis.hr

ISBN: 978-1-912545-97-1

Printed by CMP (UK), Poole, Dorset | www.cmp-uk.com

This publication is made possible by the Croatian Ministry of Culture.

Republic
of Croatia
Ministry
of Culture
Republika
Hrvatska
Ministarstvo
kulture

This book has been selected to receive financial assistance from English PEN's "PEN Translates" programme,
supported by Arts Council England. English PEN exists to promote literature and our understanding of it, to
uphold writers' freedoms around the world, to campaign against the persecution and imprisonment of writers
for stating their views, and to promote the friendly co-operation of writers and the free exchange of ideas.

www.englishpen.org